Kate A. Wright

Dainty Poems of the nineteenth Century

Kate A. Wright

Dainty Poems of the nineteenth Century

ISBN/EAN: 9783337117610

Printed in Europe, USA, Canada, Australia, Japan

Cover: Foto ©Andreas Hilbeck / pixelio.de

More available books at **www.hansebooks.com**

Dainty Poems of the Nineteenth Century

Edited by

KATE A. WRIGHT

Editor of "A Garland of
Orange Blossoms."

BIRMINGHAM : C. COMBRIDGE, NEW STREET

    ,,   C. COMBRIDGE, FIVE WAYS, EDGBASTON

DUBLIN : COMBRIDGE & CO., GRAFTON STREET

LONDON : SIMPKIN, MARSHALL, HAMILTON, KENT & CO.

First Edition, September 1895.
Second Edition, December 1895.
Third Edition, May 1898.
Fourth Edition, October 1899.

PREFACE

THE Editor's most cordial thanks are due to the following Poets and Publishers for their courtesy in giving her permission to publish the poems contained in her Anthology.

Sir EDWIN ARNOLD and Messrs LONGMANS, GREEN & Co.

Mr S. T. BADGER.

Mrs W. NICHOLSON for the late Mr EDWARD BANKS.

Mr ARTHUR C. BENSON.

"BRET HARTE" and Messrs CHATTO & WINDUS.

Mr ROBERT BRIDGES.

Mrs CALVERLEY for the late Mr C. S. CALVERLEY.

Mrs CLOUGH for the late Mr ARTHUR HUGH CLOUGH.

Mr AUSTIN DOBSON.

Mr EUGENE FIELD.

Mr NORMAN GALE.

Mr RICHARD LE GALLIENNE.

Mr EDMUND GOSSE.

Mr EUGENE LEE-HAMILTON.

Col. JOHN HAY.

Mr ALFRED HAYES.

Preface.

The late Dr OLIVER WENDELL HOLMES and
Messrs HOUGHTON & MIFFLIN.

Messrs MACMILLAN & Co. for the late Rev.
CHARLES KINGSLEY.

Messrs CHATTO & WINDUS for Dr GEORGE
MACDONALD.

Mr ERIC MACKAY.

Mrs LOUISE C. MOULTON for the late Mr
PHILIP BOURKE MARSTON.

The late Major CHARLES MAYERS.

Mrs MEYNELL and Messrs ELKIN MATTHEWS
and JOHN LANE.

Mr WILLIAM MORRIS.

Mr CRAIK for the late Miss MULOCH.

The Hon. the late RODEN NOEL.

Sir NÖEL PATON.

Messrs ELLIS & ELVEY for the late Mr DANTE
G. ROSSETTI.

Mr GEORGE ALLEN for Mr JOHN RUSKIN.

Mr WILLIAM SHARP.

Lord DE TABLEY.

Mr AUBREY DE VERE.

The PROPRIETORS, *Birmingham Daily Post.*

INTRODUCTION

THE lover of poetry is as eager to discover and to possess gems of poetical thought as are the various collectors of works of Art and Bric-a-Brac; and he has the gratification that his accumulations being stored in memory, or in manuscript, the enjoyment of his treasures may be communicated to appreciative friends.

It was in pursuit of an endeavour to save from neglect some modern poems of merit which were to be found scattered through periodicals of an evanescent character, that a manuscript collection was commenced by the Editor. This idea, however, fell out of favour through the rare occurrence of suitable matter, and it became evident that a broader, truer, and more certain field for selection might be found in the published works of living authors, or such others as have adorned English literature in the present century.

These works, however, especially some of recent publication, are too numerous and too expensive to be purchasable by the majority of readers, or too rare to be within their reach; but a judicious selection may be accessible to all.

On beginning to select from the works of recent poets the editor found that the most

Introduction.

attractive were protected by copyright. This difficulty was however overcome by the unfailing courtesy and kindness of both American and British authors, who, upon being applied to, promptly sanctioned the publication of the solicited selections from their works, as contained in the present volume.

One poem, "Monona," by the late Major Charles G. Mayers of Madison, Wisconsin, U.S.A., Poet and Dramatist, is included on account of the novelty of the subject, and its romantic and poetic quality. The Lake Monona is one of a succession of four lakes, between two of which the lovely city Madison, the seat of the Wisconsin State Government, is built.

Major Mayers wrote in similar style a romantic Indian Legendary poem on each of the other three lakes.

The lakes are named "Kegonsa" (The Fish Lake), "Wabesa" (The Lake of the White Swan), "Monona" (The Beautiful Lake), and "Mendota" (The Spirit Lake), and are continuous on the Catfish River.

The selection is submitted to the public with a confident belief that the intrinsic merit of each poem will afford so much pleasure as will excite in the reader a desire to obtain a better knowledge of the works of the different Authors of which it affords only an unsatisfying taste.

HENRY WRIGHT.

MONONA HOUSE,
SMALL HEATH, BIRMINGHAM.
August 1895.

Sir Edwin Arnold

TO A PAIR OF SLIPPERS IN THE EGYPTIAN EXHIBITION, PICCADILLY

Tiny slippers of gold and green,
  Tied with a mouldering golden cord!
What pretty feet they must have been,
  When Cæsar Augustus was Egypt's Lord!
Somebody graceful and fair you were!
  Not many girls could dance in these!
When did the shoemaker make you, dear,
  Such a nice pair of Egyptian "threes"?

Where were you measured? In Saïs, or On,
  Memphis, or Thebes, or Pelusium?—
Fitting them featly your brown toes upon,
  Lacing them deftly with finger and thumb
I seem to see you!—So long ago!
  Twenty centuries—less or more!
And here are the sandals; yet none of us know
  What name, or fortune, or face you bore!

Your lips would have laughed, with a rosy scorn,
  If the merchant or slave had mockingly said:
" The feet will pass, but the shoes they have
      worn
  Two thousand years onward Time's road shall
      tread,

A   1

And still be foot-gear, as good as new!"
   To think that calf-skin, gilded and stitched.
Should Rome and her Cæsars outlive; and you
   Be gone like a dream from the world you
      bewitched!   .

Not that we mourn you; 'twere too absurd!
   You have been such a very long while away!
Your dry spiced dust would not value a word
   Of the soft regrets that a verse could say,
Sorrow and Joy, and Love and Hate,
   If you ever felt them are vaporised hence
To this odour—subtle and delicate—
   Of cassia, and myrrh, and frankincense.

Of course they embalmed you! But not so
      sweet
   Were aloes and nard as your youthful glow
Which Amenti took, when the small dark feet
   Wearied of treading our Earth below.
Look! it was flood-time in valley of Nile,
   Or a very wet day in the Delta, dear!
When your gilded shoes tripped their latest mile,
   The mud on the soles renders that fact clear.

You knew Cleopatra no doubt! You saw,
   Antony's galleys from Actium come!
But, there!—if questions could answers draw
   From lips so many a long age dumb—
I would not tease you for history,
   Nor vex your heart with the men which were;
The one point to know that would fascinate me,
   Is, where and what are you, to-day, my dear!

2

Nineteenth Century.

You died believing in Horus and Pasht,
  Isis, Osiris, and priestly lore ;
And found of course such theories smashed
  By actual fact, on the heavenly shore !
What next did you do ? Did you transmigrate ?
  Have we seen you since, all modern and fresh ?
Your charming soul—as I calculate—
  Mislaid its mummy, and sought new flesh.

Were you she whom I met at dinner last week,
  With eyes and hair of Ptolemy black,
Who still of this " find " in the Fayoum would
    speak,
  And to scarabs and Pharaohs would carry us
    back ?
A scent of lotus around her hung,
  She had such a far-away wistful air
As of somebody born when the Earth was
    young,
  And wore of gilt slippers a lovely pair !

Perchance you were married ? These might
    have been
  Part of your trousseau—the wedding shoes ;
And you laid them aside with the lote-leaves
    green,
  And painted 'ny gods which a Bride did use :
And maybe to-day by Nile's bright waters
  Damsels of Egypt in gowns of blue—
Great — great — great — very great grand-
    daughters—
  Owe their shapely insteps to you !

3

Dainty Poems.

But vainly I knock at the bars of the past,
  Little green slippers with golden strings !
For all you can tell is that leather will last
  When loves and delights and beautiful things
Have vanished, forgotten !   Nay ! not quite
      that !
  I catch some light of the grace you wore
When you finished with life's daily pit-a-pat,
  And left your shoes at Time's bedroom door.

You were born in the Old World which did not
      doubt ;
    You were never sad with our new-fashioned
      sorrow ;
  You were sure, when your gladsome days ran
      out,
    Of day-times to come, as we of to-morrow !
Oh ! dead little maid of the Delta ! I lay
    Your shoes on your mummy-chest back again,
And wish that one game we might merrily play
    At " Hunt-the-Slipper " to see it all plain !

S. T. Badger

SLEEP

Sleep, gentle sleep! that mocks the seeker's
    toil,
And softly wraps the tiller of the soil!
Workers at night, who rack the weary brain
Seek her alas, and often seek in vain,
Have dreadful visions, dark, and weird, and
    wild;
She folds her pinions o'er the little child.

Edward Banks

"I WROTE HER NAME ON THE SAND"

I WROTE her name on the sand
  By the side of a sounding sea,
With a beating heart, and a hand
  That shook ; for it was to me
The name of the dearest girl in the land
Lovingly trac'd on the shifting sand.

A beauteous glancing line
  Of breakers bounded the beach ;
I looked on the coming brine—
  I lingered to watch it reach
The name of the dearest girl in the land
Lovingly trac'd on the yellow sand.

And just as the morning sun
  Arose in a purple mist,
With reverence, one by one,
  The ripples tenderly kissed
The name of the dearest girl in the land,
Lovingly trac'd on the shining sand.

Water of luminous green !
  Washing a lonely bay,
Whisper not what you have seen,
  What you have seen to-day—
The name of the dearest girl in the land,
Lovingly trac'd on the golden sand.

6

Dainty Poems.

Strange prophetic longing thrill'd us,
  As the sultry day-beam pass'd,
And the gather'd power of evening
  'Temper'd every hue at last.

We had heard a wondrous whisper
  Of the spirit, calm and bright,
That descends, in deep compassion,
  Unto thirsting flowers at night;

And afar to airy distance
  Was our eager gaze address'd,
Till the conquer'd flush of sunset
  Melted grandly from the west.

Dying, dying tints of purple
  Touch'd us in our dreamy bed;
Thro' the forest went the fragrance
  That her young and loveliest shed;

Softly woke a wind's enchantment,
  And the lilies, waving white,
Met it with a gentle murmur
  Of serene intense delight.

Then we felt a magic Presence
  In the hush'd elysian air,
And we look'd upon the Being
  Of our long, impassioned prayer.

Dainty Poems of the

Floating delicately downward
  From the azure-vaulted skies—
And the stars, that silver'd heaven
  Had their image in her eyes.

Rosy blooms of damask splendour
  Swing beside us, rich and tall—
We without a hint of colour—
  But she bless'd us, one and all;

Every faint and fever'd blossom,
  In the wide Hesperian grove,
Felt a touch of tender virtue
  Thro' the veil that Darkness wove;

And the voice of Slumber charm'd us
  To Oblivion's restful sphere,
And our dream was all of gladness,
  For the Spirit linger'd near.

Orient bathed in burning lustre!
  Pitiless, the summons shone,
Quench'd the visionary rapture;
  We awoke, and found her gone.

In the blinding glare we faded;
  Hours, that pass'd with winged feet,
Watch'd a drooping, sad endurance—
  Now, we perish in the heat.

Pansy, bright with opening promise—
  Pure existence, just begun!
Till the tranquil shadows lengthen,
  Thou art strong to bear the sun;

Nigh to noon, and full of freshness !
   Thou may'st see the Angel yet ;
Tell her, tell her, while we wither'd
   That we never could forget.

—>§-§<—

WEDDING WISHES

TO J. C.

HE thought upon the lonely life,
   And, pitying, spake—" It is not good."
Fair was the vision of a wife,
   In fresh-created womanhood.
A thrill of wonder and of awe
   Thro' Heaven and wide Existence ran,
That hail'd the passing into law
   His gift for Man.

And many an unremaining dream,
   And many a goal resign'd with ruth,
Are lost upon the rapid stream
   That bears us far from youth ;
But this eternal ordinance,
   Intense, as sunlight unto flowers,
Amid the ruin of Romance,
   Continueth ours.

Go forth, mine honour'd, peerless Friend
   From long-anticipative prayer
To sacred happiness, whose end
   Is not with Time—nor compass'd there ;

May loyal deed and holiest thought
   Be crown'd at length with utter bliss,
And all, that Memory knows, be naught,
   In joy, to this !

And thou, sweet Influence, reigning Queen
   O'er intellect and rarest worth,
How truly, gratefully 'twas seen
   That angels tread our shadow'd earth ;
When solemnly, about his path,
   The beauty of thy soul and face
Fell, as the charm that moon-rise hath,
   In tender grace !

Pass on together—Deep delight
   Sumless, immortal, fill your home ;
And all the rapture, promis'd, bright,
   In those first meetings by the foam
Of echoing water, now be felt !
   Endearment framed on that wild shore
A bond, whose wondrous power shall melt,
   Now, never more.

Pass on together. Nobler hearts
   Were ne'er united. Till, above,
All shall be Perfect, live your parts,
   As ye have chosen, strong in love.
Morning of June—its moments fade,
   But not the homage it has won—
Another priceless compact made,
   And Heaven begun.

TEMPUS EDAX RERUM

Love awaken'd, and Care was lighter
  Afar in an unreturning Spring ;
Were the delicate earth-hues brighter,
  Or is it a fond imagining?
When April's passionate shower was over—
  Its blue enchantment without a tear—
And sunbeams kiss'd the enamour'd clover,
  She came to meet me.   Ah, Love and Fear !

The brow was thoughtful, the eyes were saintly,
  The hair was of long and rippled gold :
I felt that my pulses flutter'd faintly,
  But that one secret was never told.
Above us, the lark attun'd his vesper,
  For what are fleeting hours to a boy?
She pass'd away like the sinking Hesper,
  But Hope was certain.   Ah, Love and Joy !

The gentle voice is in Memory's keeping ;
  The eyes are calm in the pictured past ;
Around me, the friends of youth are sleeping ;
  And earthly promise has wither'd fast.
But I often think, when the days are lonely,
  How nearly I touch'd Life's true sublime ;
Alas, it was but a vision only—
  The word unutter'd.   Ah, Love and Time !

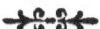

Dainty Poems.

THE SNOW-STORM

Snow, snow, feathery snow !
Falling and covering all below ;
    Never it ceases ;
    Hurrying fleeces
Fitfully, fitfully to and fro.

Snow, snow, feathery snow !
Look at the flakes how fast they go,
    Glittering brightly,
    Scattering lightly
Over the beds where the violets blow.

Snow, snow, feathery snow !
Emblem of purity fill'd with woe :
    Magical duty—
    Watch we the beauty
Of the serene and heaven-sent snow

Arthur Christopher Benson

APIS MATINA

O ORANGE-banded bee,
  Impetuously humming
You bring sweet news to me
  Of summer coming !

Here in my garden-house,
  Beside a lilac border,
I, like some prisoned mouse,
  In sick disorder,

Bewail the darkened skies,
  Pray that the flowers smell sweeter,
Wish all things otherwise,
  Slower or fleeter !

You enter with a hum
  Of warlike trumpets blowing,
You lead the months that come,
  And chase them going ;

The trembling spider stares
  Deep in his secret funnel,
Glad if your rude wing spares
  His gauzy tunnel.

Dainty Poems.

Softly, more softly, friend !
  Why such a furious pother ?
Let speed and leisure blend,
  Not slay each other !

So swift your clear wing beats,
  With hum melodious noising,
A floating aureole fleets
  Around you poising !

And where you hang in the air,
  The dust, the small things under,
Whisk swiftly here and there
  In your soft thunder.

O furred and banded bee,
  So busy, so decorous,
Would that my melody
  Were as sonorous !

Would that my days were spent
  In making sweet provision !
Would that I came and went
  With like decision !

Old minstrel, ere you go,
  To cheer the cheerless weather,
Come, let us softly blow
  One stave together !

Robert Bridges

ELEGY, ON A LADY WHOM GRIEF FOR THE DEATH OF HER BETROTHED KILLED

REACH down the wedding vesture, that has lain
Yet all unvisited, the silken gown :
Bring out the bracelets, and the golden chain
Her dearer friends provided : sere and brown
Bring out the festal crown,
And sit it on her forehead lightly :
Though it be withered, twine no wreath again ;
This only is the crown she can wear rightly.

Cloke her in ermine, for the night is cold,
And wrap her warmly, for the night is long,
In pious hands the flaming torches hold,
While her attendants, chosen from among
Her faithful virgin throng,
May lay her in her cedar litter,
Decking her coverlet with sprigs of gold,
Roses, and lilies white that best befit her.

Sound flute and tabor, that the bridal be
Not without music, nor with these alone ;
But let the viol lead the melody,
With lesser intervals, and plaintive moan

Of sinking semitone ;
And, all in choir, the virgin voices
Rest not from singing in skilled harmony
The song that aye the bridegroom's ear rejoices.

Let the priests go before, arrayed in white,
And let the dark stoled minstrels follow slow,
Next they that bear her, honoured on this night,
And then the maidens, in a double row,
Each singing soft and low,
And each on high a torch upstaying :
Unto her lover lead her forth with light,
With music, and with singing, and with praying.

-->&-3<--

I WILL NOT LET THEE GO

I WILL not let thee go.
Ends all our month-long love in this?
Can it be summed up so,
Quit in a single kiss?
I will not let thee go.

I will not let thee go.
If thy words' breath could scare thy deeds,
As the soft south can blow
And toss the feathered seeds,
Then might I let thee go.

I will not let thee go.
Had not the great sun seen, I might ;
Or were he reckoned slow
To bring the false to light,
Then might I let thee go.

16

Nineteenth Century.

I will not let thee go.
The stars that crowd the summer skies
Have watched us so below
With all their million eyes,
I dare not let thee go.

I will not let thee go.
Have we not chid the changeful moon,
Now rising late, and now
Because she set too soon,
And shall I let thee go?

I will not let thee go.
Have not the young flowers been content,
Plucked ere their buds could blow,
To seal our sacrament?
I cannot let thee go.

I will not let thee go.
I hold thee by too many bands:
Thou sayest farewell, and lo!
I have thee by the hands,
And will not let thee go.

Mrs E. B. Browning

A WOMAN'S SHORTCOMINGS

I.

She has laughed as softly as if she sighed ;
  She has counted six and over,
Of a purse well filled, and a heart well tried—
  Oh, each a worthy lover !
They "give her time ;" for her soul must slip
  Where the world has set the grooving :
She will lie to none with her fair red lip—
  . But love seeks truer loving.

II.

She trembles her fan in a sweetness dumb,
  As her thoughts were beyond recalling ;
With a glance for *one*, and a glance for *some*,
  From her eyelids rising and falling.
—Speaks common words with a blushful air ;
  —Hears bold words, unreproving :
But her silence says—what she never will
    swear—
  And love seeks better loving.

III.

Go, lady ! lean to the night-guitar,
  And drop a smile to the bringer ;
Then smile as sweetly, when he is far,
  At the voice of an in-door singer !

Bask tenderly beneath tender eyes ;
  Glance lightly, on their removing ;
And join new vows to old perjuries—
  But dare not call it loving !

IV.

Unless you can think, when the song is done,
  No other is soft in the rhythm ;
Unless you can feel, when left by one,
  That all men else go with him ;
Unless you can know, when unpraised by his
      breath,
  That your beauty itself wants proving ;
Unless you can swear—" For life, for death "—
  Oh, fear to call it loving !

V.

Unless you can muse in a crowd all day,
  On the absent face that fixed you ;
Unless you can love as the angels may,
  With the breadth of heaven betwixt you ;
Unless you can dream that his faith is fast,
  Through behooving and unbehooving ;
Unless you can die when the dream is past—
  Oh, never call it loving !

SONG

WEEP, as if you thought of laughter !
Smile, as tears were coming after !
Marry your pleasures to your woes ;
And think life's green well worth its rose !

No sorrow will your heart betide,
Without a comfort by its side ;
The sun may sleep in his sea-bed,
But you have starlight over-head.

Trust not to joy ! the rose of June,
When opened wide, will wither soon ;
Italian days without twilight,
Will turn them suddenly to night.

Joy, most changeful of all things,
Flits away on rainbow wings ;
And when they look the gayest, know,
It is that they are spread to go !

SONNET

First time he kissed me, he but only kissed
The fingers of this hand wherewith I write,
And ever since it grew more clean and
    white, ...
Slow to world-greetings . . . quick with its
    " Oh list ! "
When the angels speak.   A ring of Amethyst
I could not wear here plainer to my sight,
Than that first kiss.   The second passed in
    height
The first, and sought the forehead, and half
    missed,
Half falling on the hair.   O beyond meed !
That was the chrism of love, which love's own
    crown,

Nineteenth Century.

With sanctifying sweetness, did precede.
The third, upon my lips, was folded down
In perfect purple state ! since when, indeed,
I have been proud, and said, " My love, my
    own."

C. S. Calverley

LOVERS, AND A REFLECTION

In moss-prankt dells which the sunbeams
flatter
(And heaven it knoweth what that may mean :
Meaning, however, is no great matter)
  Where woods are a-tremble, with rifts atween;

Thro' God's own heather we wonn'd together,
  I and my Willie (O love my love :)
I need hardly remark it was glorious weather,
  And flitterbats waver'd alow, above :

Boats were curtseying, rising, bowing,
  (Boats in that climate are so polite),
And sands were a ribbon of green endowing,
  And O the sun-dazzle on bark and bight !

Thro' the rare red heather we danced together,
  (O love my Willie !) and smelt for flowers :
I must mention again it was gorgeous weather,
  Rhymes are so scarce in this world of ours :—

By rises that flush'd with their purple favours,
  Thro' becks that brattled o'er grasses sheen,
We walked and waded, we two young shavers,
  Thanking our stars we were both so green.

Dainty Poems

We journeyed in parallels, I and Willie,
  In fortunate parallels !   Butterflies,
Hid in weltering shadows of daffodilly
  Or marjoram, kept making peacock eyes :

Songbirds darted about, some inky
  As coal, some snowy (I ween) as curds ;
Or rosy as pinks, or as roses pinky—
  They reck of no eerie To-come, those birds !

But they skim over bents which the millstream
      washes,
  Or hang in the lift 'neath a white cloud's hem ;
They need no parasols, no goloshes ;
  And good Mrs Trimmer she feedeth them.

Then we thrid God's cowslips (as erst His
      heather)
  That endowed the wan grass with their
      golden blooms ;
And   snapt — (it   was   perfectly   charming
      weather)—
  Our fingers at Fate and her goddess-
      glooms :

And Willie 'gan sing (O his notes were fluty ;
  Wafts fluttered them out to the white-wing'd
      sea)—
Something made up of rhymes that have done
      much duty,
  Rhymes (better to put it) of " ancientry " :

Dainty Poems.

Bowers of flowers encounter'd showers
   In William's carol—(O love my Willie!)
Then he bade sorrow borrow from blithe to-
      morrow
   I quite forget what—say a daffodilly:

A nest in a hollow, "with buds to follow,"
   I think occurred next in his nimble strain;
And clay that was "kneaden" of course in
      Eden—
   A rhyme most novel, I do maintain:

Mists, bones, the singer himself, love-stories,
   And all least furlable things got "furled";
Not with any design to conceal their "glories,"
   But simply and solely to rhyme with "world."

     ·   ·   ·   ·   ·

O if billows and pillows and hours and flowers,
   And all the brave rhymes of an elder day,
Could be furled together, this genial weather,
   And carted, or carried on "wafts" away,
Nor ever again trotted out—ah me!
How much fewer volumes of verse there'd be!

Will Carleton

ONE AND TWO

If you to me be cold,
Or I be false to you,
The world will go on, I think,
Just as it used to do ;
The clouds will flirt with the moon,
The sun will kiss the sea,
The winds to the trees will whisper,
And laugh at you and me.
But the sun will not shine so bright,
The clouds will not seem so white,
To one as they will to two ;
So I think you had better be kind,
And I had best be true,
And let the old love go on,
Just as it used to do.

If the whole of a page be read,
If a book be finished through,
Still the world may read on, I think,
Just as it used to do ;
For other lovers will con
The pages we have passed,
And the treacherous gold of binding
Will glitter unto the last.

But lids have a lonely book,
And one may not read the book,
It opens only to two ;
So I think you had better be kind,
And I had best be true,
And let the reading go on
Just as it used to do.

If we who have sailed together
Flit out of each other's view,
The world will sail on, I think,
Just as it used to do ;
And we may reckon by stars
That flash from different skies,
And another of Love's pirates
May capture my prize.
But ships long time together
Can better the tempest weather
Than any other two ;
So I think you had better be kind
And I had best be true,
That we may together sail
Just as we used to do.

--*--

SOME TIME

O STRONG and terrible Ocean,
O grand and glorious Ocean,
O restless, stormy Ocean, a million fathoms o'er !
When never an eye was near thee to view thy
turbulent glory,
When never an ear to hear thee relate thy
endless story,

Nineteenth Century.

What did'st thou then, O Ocean? Did'st toss
    thy foam in air,
With never a bark to fear thee, and never a
    soul to dare?

      "Oh, I was the self-same Ocean,
        The same majestic Ocean,
The strong and terrible Ocean, with rock-em-
    battled shore;
I threw my fleecy blanket up over my shoul-
    ders bare,
I raised my head in triumph, and tossed my
    grizzled hair;
For I knew that some time—some time—
White-robed ships would venture from out of
    the placid bay,
Forth to my heaving bosom, my lawful pride
    or prey;
I knew that some time—some time—
Lordly men and maidens my servile guests
    would be,
And hearts of sternest courage would falter
    and bend to me."

      O deep and solemn Forest,
      O sadly whispering Forest,
O lonely moaning Forest, that murmureth
    evermore!
When never a footstep wandered across thy
    sheltered meadows,
When never a wild-bird squandered his music
    'mid thy shadows,
What did'st thou then, O Forest? Did'st robe
    thyself in green,
And pride thyself in beauty the while to be unseen?

"Oh, I was the self-same Forest,
 The same low-whispering Forest,
The softly-murmuring Forest, and all of my
 beauties wore.
I dressed myself in splendour all through the
 lonely hours ;
I twined the vines around me, and covered my
 lap with flowers ;
For I knew that some time—some time—
Birds of beautiful plumage would flit and nestle
 here ;
Songs of marvellous sweetness would charm
 my listening ear ;
I knew that some time—some time—
Lovers would gaily wander 'neath my protect-
 ing boughs,
And into the ear of my silence would whisper
 holy vows."

 O fair and beautiful Maiden,
 O poor and winsome Maiden,
O grand and peerless Maiden, created to adore !
When no love came to woo thee that won thy
 own love-treasure,
When never a heart came to thee thy own heart-
 wealth could measure,
What did'st thou then, O Maiden? Did'st
 smile as thou smilest now,
With ne'er the kiss of a lover upon thy snow-
 white brow ?

 "Oh, I was the self-same Maiden,
 The simple and trusting Maiden,
The happy and careless Maiden, with all of
 my love in store.

Nineteenth Century.

I gaily twined my tresses, and cheerfully went
    my way :
I took no thought of the morrow, and cared
    for the cares of the day ;
For I knew that some time—some time—
Into the path of my being the love of my life
    would glide,
And we by the gates of heaven would wander
    side by side."

Arthur Hugh Clough

AN INCIDENT

'Twas on a sunny summer day
  I trod a mighty city's street,
And when I started on my way
  My heart was full of fancies sweet;
But soon, as nothing could be seen,
But countenances sharp and keen,
Nought heard or seen around but told
Of something bought or something sold,
And none that seemed to think or care
That any save himself was there,—

Full soon my heart began to sink
  With a strange shame and inward pain,
For I was sad within to think
  Of this absorbing love of gain,
And various thoughts my bosom tost;
When suddenly my path there crossed,
Locked hand in hand with one another,
A little maiden and her brother—
A little maiden, and she wore
Around her waist a pinafore.

And hand in hand along the street
  This pretty pair did softly go,
And as they went, their little feet
  Moved in short even steps and slow:

It was a sight to see and bless,
That little sister's tenderness;
One hand a tidy basket bore
Of flowers and fruit—a chosen store,
Such as kind friends oft send to others—
And one was fastened in her brother's.

It was a voice of meaning sweet,
  And spake amid that scene of strife
Of home and homely duties meet,
  And charities of daily life;
And often, should my spirit fail,
And under cold strange glances quail,
'Mid busy shops and busier throng,
That speed upon their ways along
The thick and crowded thoroughfare
I'll call to mind that little pair.

⟶⊱⊰⟵

LAST WORDS. NAPOLEON AND WELLINGTON.

NAPOLEON.

Is it this, then, O world-warrior,
  That, exulting, through the folds
Of the dark and cloudy barrier
  Thine enfranchised eye beholds?
Is, when blessed hands relieve thee
  From the gross and mortal clay,
This the heaven that should receive thee?
          " Tête d'armée."

Now the final link is breaking,
  Of the fierce, corroding chain,
And the ships, their watch forsaking,
  Bid the seas no more detain,
Whither is it, freed and risen,
  The pure spirit seeks away,
Quits for what the weary prison ?
                "Tête d'armée."

Doubtless—angels, hovering o'er thee
  In thine exile's sad abode,
Marshalled even now before thee,
  Move upon that chosen road !
Thither they, ere friends have laid thee
  Where sad willows o'er thee play,
Shall already have conveyed thee !
                "Tête d'armée."

Shall great captains, foiled and broken,
  Hear from thee on each great day,
At the crisis, a word spoken—
  Word that battles still obey—
"Cuirassiers here, here those cannon ;
  Quick those squadrons, up—away !
To the charge, on—as one man, on !"
                "Tête d'armée."

(Yes, too true, alas ! while sated
  Of the wars so slow to cease,
Nations, once that scorned and hated,
  Would to Wisdom turn, and Peace ;
Thy dire impulse still obeying,
  Fevered youths, as in the old day,
In their hearts still find thee saying,
                "Tête d'armée.")

Nineteenth Century.

Oh, poor soul!—or do I view thee,
   From earth's battle-fields withheld,
In a dream, assembling to thee
   Troops that quell not nor are quelled,
Breaking airy lines, defeating
   Limbo-kings, and, as to-day,
Idly to all time repeating
              " Tête d'armée.'

WELLINGTON.

And what the words, that with his failing breath
   Did England hear her aged soldier say?
I know not.   Yielding tranquilly to death,
   With no proud speech, no boast, he passed
      away.

Not stirring words, nor gallant deeds alone,
   Plain patient work fulfilled that length of life;
Duty, not glory—Service, not a throne,
   Inspired his effort, set for him the strife.

Therefore just Fortune, with one hasty blow,
   Spurning her minion, Glory's, Victory's lord,
Gave all to him that was content to know,
   In service done its own supreme reward.

The words he said, if haply words there were,
   When full of years and works he passed away,
Most naturally might, methinks, refer
   To some poor humble business of to-day.

" That humble, simple duty of the day
   Perform," he bids; " ask not if small or great:
Serve in thy post; be faithful, and obey;
   Who serves her truly, sometimes saves the
      state."

C   33

Austin Dobson

AN AUTUMN IDYLL

"Sweet Themmes! runne softly, till I end my song."—SPENSER.

LAWRENCE.   FRANK.   JACK.

LAWRENCE.

Here, where the beech-nuts drop among the
    grasses,
  Push the boat in, and throw the rope ashore.
Jack, hand me out the claret and the glasses;
  Here let us sit.   We landed here before.

FRANK.

Jack's undecided.   Say, *formose puer*,
  Bent in a dream above the " water wan,"
Shall we row higher, for the reeds are fewer
  There by the pollards, where you see the
    swan?

JACK.

Hist !   That's a pike.   Look—nose against the
  river,
  Gaunt as a wolf,—the sly old privateer !
Enter a gudgeon.   Snap,—a gulp, a shiver ;—
  Exit the gudgeon.   Let us anchor here.

Dainty Poems.

FRANK (*in the grass*).

Jove, what a day ! Black Care upon the crupper
  Nods at his post, and slumbers in the sun ;
Half of Theocritus, with a touch of Tupper,
  Churns in my head. The frenzy has begun !

LAWRENCE.

Sing to us then. Damoetas in a choker,
  Much out of tune, will edify the rooks.

FRANK.

Sing you again. So musical a croaker
  Surely will draw the fish upon the hooks.

JACK.

Sing while you may. The beard of manhood
      still is
Faint on your cheeks, but I, alas ! am old.
Doubtless you yet believe in Amaryllis ;—
  Sing me of Her, whose name may not be told.

FRANK.

Listen, O Thames ! His budding beard is riper,
  Say—by a week. Well, Lawrence, shall we
      sing ?

LAWRENCE.

Yes, if you will. But ere I play the piper,
  Let him declare the prize he has to bring.

JACK.

Hear then, my Shepherds. Lo, to him
      accounted
  First in the song, a Pipe I will impart ;—
This, my Belovèd, marvellously mounted,
  Amber and foam, a miracle of art.

35

LAWRENCE.

Lordly the gift.   O muse of many numbers,
  Grant me a soft alliterative song !

FRANK.

Me too, O Muse !   And when the Umpire
    slumbers,
  Sting him with gnats a summer evening long.

LAWRENCE.

Not in a cot, begarlanded of spiders,
  Not where the brook traditionally " purls,"—
No, in the Row, supreme among the riders,
  Seek I the gem,—the paragon of girls.

FRANK.

Not in the waste of column and of coping,
  Not in the sham and stucco of a square,—
No, on a June-lawn, to the water sloping,
  Stands she I honour, beautifully fair.

LAWRENCE.

Dark-haired is mine, with splendid tresses
    plaited
  Back from the brows, imperially curled ;
Calm as a grand, far-looking Caryatid,
  Holding the roof that covers in a world.

FRANK.

Dark-haired is mine, with breezy ripples
    swinging
  Loose as a vine-branch blowing in the morn ;
Eyes like the morning, mouth for ever singing,
  Blithe as a bird new risen from the corn.

Nineteenth Century.

LAWRENCE.

Best is the song with music interwoven :
  Mine's a musician,—musical at heart,—
Throbs to the gathered grieving of Beethoven,
  Sways to the light coquetting of Mozart.

FRANK.

Best? You should hear mine trilling out a
    ballad,
  Queen at a pic-nic, leader of the glees,
Not too divine to toss you up a salad,
  Great in Sir Roger danced among the trees.

LAWRENCE.

Ah, when the thick night flares with drooping
    torches,
  Ah, when the crush-room empties of the
    swarm,
Pleasant the hand that, in the gusty porches,
  Light as a snow-flake, settles on your arm.

FRANK.

Better the twilight and the cheery chatting,—
  Better the dim, forgotten garden-seat,
Where one may lie, and watch the fingers
    tatting,
  Lounging with Bran or Bevis at her feet.

LAWRENCE.

All worship mine. Her purity doth hedge her
  Round with so delicate divinity, that men,
Stained to the soul with money-bag and ledger,
  Bend to the goddess, manifest again.

FRANK.

None worship mine. But some, I fancy, love
     her,—
  Cynics to boot.   I know the children run,
Seeing her come, for naught that I discover,
  Save that she brings the summer and the sun.

LAWRENCE.

Mine is a Lady, beautiful and queenly,
  Crowned with a sweet, continual control,
Grandly forbearing, lifting life serenely
  E'en to her own nobility of soul.

FRANK.

Mine is a Woman, kindly beyond measure,
  Fearless in praising, faltering in blame :
imply devoted to other people's pleasure,—
  Jack's sister Florence,—now you know her
     name.

LAWRENCE.

"Jack's sister Florence!" Never, Francis, never.
  Jack, do you bear ? Why, it was she I meant.
She like the country ! Ah, she's far too clever—

FRANK.

  There you are wrong. I knew her down in
     Kent.

LAWRENCE.

You'll get a sunstroke, standing with your head
     bare.
  Sorry to differ. Jack,—the word's with you.

Nineteenth Century.

FRANK.

How is it, Umpire? Though the motto's
   threadbare,
  "Coelum, non animum "—is, I take it, true.

JACK.

"Souvent femme varie," as a rule, is truer ;
  Flattered, I'm sure, — but both of you
   romance.
Happy to further suit of either wooer,
  Merely observing—you haven't got a chance.

LAWRENCE.

Yes. But the Pipe—

FRANK.

     The Pipe is what we care for,—

JACK.

Well, in this case, I scarcely need explain,
Judgment of mine were indiscreet, and there-
   fore,—
  Peace to you both.   The Pipe I shall retain.

Mrs H. V. Elliott

SONGS WITHOUT WORDS

Mendelssohn said of the following lines when they were read to him, " Many have tried before to express what they fancied I meant to convey in that Music, 'Songs without Words.' but no one has ever before succeeded in putting into words the thoughts and feelings which were in my own mind so nearly as this poem does."

Sing no words to-night,
   But play that air for me,
While I, in calm delight,
   Sit musing silently.

That soft, low, murm'ring air,
   With its solemn wavelike swell :
There are hidden meanings there
   Which words may never tell.

The heart has secret cells
   And mines of ore unwrought,
Where many a treasure dwells
   Of never-utter'd thought.

Sweet the poet's song
   Clothed in its finish'd grace,
When the numbers roll along
   With proud and measured pace.

Dainty Poems.

But it seem'd more sweet to him
  When it floated on his ear,
Like marbled echoes dim
  From a spirit-haunted sphere.

Fair may be the form
  Shaped by the painter's hand,
When in breathing beauty warm
  We see the image stand.

But to him it seem'd more fair
  When it gleamed upon his eye,
A radiant thing of air,
  Which he worshipp'd silently.

Nought may ever be
  So beautiful, so blest,
As the first virgin sanctity
  Of feelings unexpressed.

We read them in the gaze
  Of some beloved eye,
Where the spirit's sunbeam plays,
  And we watch it gleam and die.

But their charms we may not tell,
  They are sullied by a breath :
They are like a fairy spell
  Which in utterance perisheth.

Then sing no words to-night,
  Or sing them with thine eyes,
While I in mute delight
  Shape mine own phantasies.

Eugene Field

DUTCH LULLABY

Wynken, Blynken, and Nod, one night
Sailed off in a wooden shoe—
Sailed on a river of crystal light
Into a sea of dew:
"Where are you going, and what do you wish?"
The old moon asked the three ;—
"We have come to fish for the herring fish
That live in this beautiful sea ;
Nets of silver and gold have we ! "
      Said Wynken,
      Blynken,
      And Nod.

The old man laughed and sang a song,
As they rocked in the wooden shoe,
And the wind that spec them all night long
Ruffled the waves of dew.
The little stars were the herring fish
That lived in that beautiful sea ;—
"Now cast your nets wherever you wish—
Never afeared are we ; "
So cried the stars to the fishermen three ;
      Wynken,
      Blynken,
      And Nod.

Dainty Poems.

All night long their nets they threw
To the stars in the twinkling foam—
Then down from the skies came the wooden
     shoe,
Bringing the fishermen home ;
'Twas all so pretty a sail, it seemed
As if it could not be,
And some folks thought 'twas a dream they'd
     dreamed
Of sailing that beautiful sea ;—
But I shall name you the fishermen three ;
       Wynken,
       Blynken,
       And Nod.

Wynken and Blynken are two little eyes,
And Nod is a little head,
And the wooden shoe that sailed the skies
Is a wee one's trundle bed.
So shut your eyes while mother sings
Of wonderful sights that be,
And you shall see the beautiful things,
As you rock in the misty sea
Where the old shoe rocked the fishermen three;
       Wynken,
       Blynken,
       And Nod.

Norman R. Gale

IN THE GLADE

From bush to bush I followed her,
  A bird that piped and flew beyond,
I saw the little branches stir,
  I saw her shadow in the pond;

And still she lured me to the wood
  With cunning notes so round and ripe:
I followed in a dreamy mood
  This feathered Orpheus and her pipe.

We passed a slope where cowslips shook
  Their yellow blossoms in the breeze;
We passed the shallows of the brook,
  And reached the temple of the trees:

And still her music onward went
  Through hazel-alleys, beechen groves,
Where doves with lulling voices sent
  Soft salutations to their loves.

So down these verdant colonnades
  I still pursued the woodland note,
O'er lawny islands of the glades
  That echoed to the blackbird's throat.

And as I neared one bright expanse,
  A cool oasis clothed with green,
A perfume, sweeter than romance—
  Than love that only might have been,

Came, with a stripling breeze for aid,
  To stay a moment, stay and pass ;
Another step.   I spied a maid,
  Or goddess, sleeping in the grass.

Around her in an amber stream
  There flowed the marvel of her hair,
The ransom for a world, the dream
  To fill the morning with despair :

The pink of apple-bloom possessed
  The virgin cheeks unkissed by man ;
And round her throat the sun had pressed
  To clasp it with his ring of tan :

Her lips, half opened, had the light
  Of cherries bathed by drops of rain ;
Reproachless was the dome of white
  Unblemished brow without a stain.

Then in my heart that love did cry,
  Which from my life shall never pass ;
And bitterly I longed to lie
  Beside her beauty in the grass.

The doves in spires of elm and oak
  Cooed softly in the afternoon,
And sometimes, from a bush there broke
  A whitethroat's tenderness of tune.

The air was full of nameless joy!
  And, daring all, I threw me down
As innocently as a boy,
  Beside her scented film of gown.

Now if some secret charm in her
  Across my aching heart did sweep,
Some magic in her bosom's stir,
  I know not—but I fell asleep,

And when the day, a patient bride,
  Was parting from her love, the sun,
The girl, or goddess, from my side,
  Had gently risen, and was gone!

—➤℈·3·◄—

GONE INTO LONG FROCKS

She's a woman!
The gracious girl's in longer dresses,
And desecrating hands have piled
In one bright crown her flying tresses;
But yesterday she was a child,
And joined to mine her frank caresses,
Perched in a pretty pose upon my knee
To stroke my face or kiss it suddenly.

She's a woman!
O thievish time, to steal my pleasure,
Her weight, her fingers in my hair!
No more she dangles at her leisure

46

A shapely limb from out the pear.
Still in a statelier way this treasure
Colours my life, and from the tomboy age
Saves me her eyes and voice for heritage.

—>§-2<—

MY CHERRY-TREES

O CHILDREN of the smoke and fog,
  With faces pinched by early care,
Would God you might adventure forth
  To breathe this country air !
Would God your ears might drink the song
  Of grasses, birds, and singing trees !
Would God your eyes grew round to see
  My wealth of cherry-trees !

A hundred thousand shining lamps
  To light the glory of the green !
The rubies of my orchard hang
  The sturdy leaves between ;
The blackbird pecks them at his will,
  The brazen sparrow with his beak
Attacks some swaying globe of fruit,
  And stabs its ruddy cheek.

But in the Covent Garden roads
  You see the sluttish cabbage-leaf
In air that steals away your strength,
  God's bounty turned a thief !
How happy is my growing boy
  That here in grass which pricks his knees
He roams his world so shy and clean
  Beneath my cherry-trees !

I often lift him to a branch
    That burns with cherries redly ripe ;
A startled thrush in flight displays
    The shrillness of her pipe ;
And down to mother's upturned mouth
    His baby hand so plumply fair
He reaches full of fruit, or drops
    A cherry in her hair !

Apollo gave my rustic Muse
    Her artless shepherd-songs to sing ;
The sorrel charms her, and the gloss
    Upon the swallow's wing ;
But often dreaming in the wood,
    When comes the evening gift of dew,
Her soul flies forward to your souls,
    And, children, thinks of you.

Your naked feet within this grass
    Should learn some simple country dance ;
Upon your hearts should flash at last
    The colours of romance.
O empty purse of mine, alas
    That such a happy vision flees !
That all these urchins may not romp
    Beneath my cherry-trees !

—➤⁙⬦—

SPRING

WHAT did Spring-time whisper ?

    O ye rivulets
Waking from your trance so sad,
Pleased to welcome fisher-lad
    With his little nets,

Nineteenth Century.

Speed, for summer's in the air,
Prattle, for the breeze is warm,
Chatter by the otter's lair,
Bubble past the ivied farm ;
Wake the primrose on the banks,
Bid the violet ope her eyes,
Hurry in a flood of thanks
Underneath serener skies !
What a revel's coming soon—
Fairies trooping o'er the leas,
Making magic by the moon,
Crowned with wood anemones !
What a haunted heart the thrush
Nurses in the blackthorn bush,
Full of splendid songs to sing,
Cheery welcomes of the Spring—
        Spring has come !

SUMMER

What was Summer chanting?

O ye brooks and birds,
Flash and pipe in happiness
Stirring hearts that cares oppress
        Into shining words !
Here's a maze of butterflies
Dancing over golden gorse,
Here's a host of grassy spies
Sunshine has set free, of course !

Wonder at the wind that blows
Odours from the forest sweet ;
Marvel at the honey'd rose
Heaping petals at her feet ;
Hark at wood-nymphs rustling through
Brakes and thickets, tender knee'd !
Hark ! some shepherd pipe there blew !
Was it Pan upon a reed ?
Oh, the pinks and garden-spice,
Nature's ev'ry fair device,
Mingled in a scented hoard
Expected, longed for and adored—
Summer's come !

AUTUMN

Wнат did Autumn murmur ?

O ye sheaves of gold
Gathered in the sun-burnt field
Where the sowing-labours yield
Treasures manifold,
Here's a jug of rare old ale
Beading still the reaper's beard,
While he whistles down the vale
As the humming farm is neared !
What a saucy knot of maids
Eggs him on to kiss his prize !
What a pack of bouncing jades
Binds a kerchief o'er his eyes—

Twirls him thrice, and bids him search
Whom he may the while they pinch,
Prick, and leave him in the lurch,
Each one shrilling like a finch !
Ah, the starlight country dance,
Not without its rough romance—
Not without the fiddle's beat
Speeding Cicely's flashing feet—
       Autumn's come !

WINTER

Wʜᴀᴛ did Winter mutter?

    O ye frozen ponds
Ring, as on the flying skate
Rapid couples, maid and mate,
    Skim in cosy bonds !
Bless me, what a scarlet nose
Comes with Robin home from school !
How his pilot jacket shows
Ghosts of snowballs on the wool !
Here are drifts beside the door,
Flakes that melt on Laura's face,
Shameless hurricanes that roar
Anger into ev'ry place !
Here's a splendid pavement-slide
Made by pourings from the jugs ;
Even babies take a pride
Helping with their china mugs !

Now's the hour when chestnuts roast,
Now for father's promised ghost !
Children, Winter's come anew—
Love him, for he worships you !
　　Winter's come !

A THRUSH IN SEVEN DIALS

Here in this den of smoke and filth
　　They caged a thrush's broken heart ;
Yet when the sun, as if by stealth,
　　Shone, or a milkman's rattling cart
Shook all her narrow wickerwork
　　The bird would chirp, and very soon
To passing Jew or Dane or Turk
　　Sing some remembered forest-tune.

But Ah, the rounded notes that rung
　　In emulation of her mate
Who in the shadowed evening sung
　　Beside the five-barred spinney-gate
Were thin and false ; but still the song
　　Gained pathos from its lessened spell,
For this proclaimed aloud the wrong
　　Of shutting thrushes up in hell !

But sometimes stirred to quite forget
　　The crime of her captivity,
The songster o'er the city's fret
　　Flung strains of bird-divinity,

52

Nineteenth Century.

And tried to stretch her tattered wings,
  And poise above the constant perch,
And answered the imaginings
  Of sparrows on the murky church.

She marvelled much that they so small,
  So scant of music, plainly drest,
Should swoop at will from wall to wall
  While she whose melody and breast
Had fluttered whitethroats in the wood
  Should hang upon a rusty nail
And chirp to great-eyed boys who stood
  To hear her sing in rain or hail !

"Twas when these urchins flocked around
  That most forgetful of her cage
Her wild wood carollings she found
  Warm in her heart, untouched by age:
So sitting on her perch she sang
  Marsh-marigolds and river-sand
Till all the grimy district rang
  With tales of moss and meadow-land.

And then for days she would not shake
  A single utterance from her store
Despite the outcast imps who spake
  Like *Oliver*, and asked for more !
In fluffy listlessness she sat
  And dreamed of all the grassy west—
How she had feared the parson's cat,
  And how she built her earliest nest !

Sometimes a French piano hurled
  Metallic scales adown the street,
That seemed to buffet all the world,
  So hard and clear, so shrill and fleet !

Dainty Poems of the

No maddened music of this kind
    Could tempt the thrush to rivalry ;
She pecked an inch of apple-rind
    And waited till the din went by !

There from a tiny patch of sun
    She made an April for her heart !
Imagined twigs, and sat thereon
    Though shaken by the milkman's cart !
The slinking fog that filled her cage
    Usurped her heritage of dew,
Of grass, of berries—all the wage
    Of hedgerows where she hid or flew.

And if perchance disdain or pride
    Made e'en her scanty chantings fail,
Sing, bird ! an ugly villain cried,
    And swung her fiercely on her nail !
This was the man whose crafty net
    Cast o'er the lilac meshed her wings—
Ah, not for such her music set
    The song of her imaginings !

Oh, leave them in the wilderness,
    Or in the bush or in the brake ;
Let them in liberty possess
    The haunts God fashioned for their sake !
And all the glories of their throats
    Shall sound more glorious when they rise
In flights and waves of noble notes
    To stir your hearts and dim your eyes.

Nineteenth Century.

THE CLOSING OF PARADISE

THE Gods who toss their bounties down
　　　　To willing laps
To some gave villas nested high
Among the foliage of the sky
Of Alps or soaring Apennine;
To some a Sabine farm; to some
The pillared porches of a home
With marble vaults for priceless wine,
And slaves whose solemn ebon line
Salutes the great who go and come.

The Gods who toss their bounties down
　　　　To willing laps
To some sent all felicities
Of native statues, foreign frieze,
And gold to bribe the poet's lyre;
To some upon the inland sea
A pleasure-ship near Sicily
Where harps and echoes long have rung,
And bards in busy vineyards sung
For maidens purple to the knee;

The Gods who toss their bounties down
　　　　To willing laps
Gave me the joy of being free—
Gave me the gift of poverty!
No eagle, sinking from the sun
At eventime, discerns afar
The flashing of a golden star
On roof of mine, nor slaves who press
With all the pomp of slavishness
To help me from my gilded car.

The Gods who toss their bounties down
　　　To willing laps
Gave me no treasure-house of pearls,
No bevy of slim dancing girls,
But finer gifts out-shining these—
A little wood whose paths are few,
Some trees made bright with fruit and dew;
And lastly, O my child so fair
With masses of resplendent hair,
They, gracious, dowered me with you!

The Gods who toss their bounties down
　　　To willing laps
Exalted me beyond my kind
With all the mercies of a mind
That does not hungry gape for change.
The blackbird of a yesterday,
So it unlearns no liquid lay,
To-morrow can entice my feet
As pilgrims after piping sweet
Across the drying lines of hay.

The Gods who toss their bounties down
　　　To willing laps
To her who left a stately house
To comfort me gave marvellous
Rare graces of pure maidenhood :
A benediction was her face,
Her heart a very tender place
Where love conceived the potent rule
To ache for others, merciful
Beyond the boundaries of race.

Nineteenth Century.

The Gods who toss their bounties down
      To willing laps
Instilled in her the simple taste
Of seeking in a country waste
For Nature's hidden handiwork :
She knew all secrets of the sedge,
The " Lords and Ladies" in the hedge,
What stripling blackbird first essayed
To fly from home, and half-dismayed
Piped pitiful upon the edge.

The Gods who toss their bounties down
      To willing laps
In uncontrolled abundancy
Decreed that praise of bud and bee
Should be the duty of her lips.
The thunder of the world roared on
Nor shook our stars that nightly won
The worship of our eager eyes
Sweeping the kingdom of the skies
Deserted by the westward sun.

The Gods who toss their bounties down
      To willing laps
Conspired to mould a million shapes—
Crocus and grasses, seas and capes—
To wake deep echoes in our hearts.
What rare divine imaginings
Conceived the ivy-spray that clings
To other miracles, the trees !
How magical those great decrees
That sent us roses, birds, and springs !

The Gods who toss their bounties down
        To willing laps
Neither forgot the violet's scent,
Nor planets in the firmament—
The outposts of a mystery !
They gave to man the undefiled
Bright rivulets and waters wild ;
They wrought at goodly gifts above,
And, for the pinnacle of love,
They fashioned him a little child.

The Gods who toss their bounties down
        To willing laps
Remembered, and a wailing cry
Smote at my heart so tenderly—
The master-miracle was ours !
He prospered in his tiny bed,
And when my angel bent her head
Translating all his uncouth cries
By knowledge motherhood supplies
My penitence arose and fled.

The Gods who toss their bounties down
        To willing laps
All suddenly announced a hate
Of me, my wood, my simple gate,
The glory of my cherry-trees !
But when for grief I scarce could speak,
Love, coming closer, kissed my cheek,
And, with the genius of caress,
By pretty acts of tenderness
Made peace more near and earth less bleak.

Nineteenth Century.

The Gods who toss their bounties down
   To willing laps
Thought, as they bent from heaven to see
This man is happier than we.
Nor were these grasping Gods ashamed
To steal from me my Love's caress,
And her, the fount of happiness,
Rainbow and sunshine of my soul
Till all embittered nations roll
Where gods nor curse again nor bless!

Ah, silent melodies of joy,
   So sadly dumb!
Ah, for the wilderness of life
With no oasis, lasting strife
With love's triumphant memory!
The memory of her! Ye great,
Who mock me and my rustic gate,
1 am the rich man of you all!
What is a polished silver wall
Compared with her who died of late?

A CREED

GOD sends no message by me. I am mute
When Wisdom crouches in her furthest cave;
I love the organ, but must touch the lute.

I cannot salve the sores of those who bleed;
I break no idols, smite no olden laws,
And come before you with no separate creed.

Dainty Poems of the

No controversies thrust me to the ledge
Of dangerous schools and doctrines hard to
    learn—
Give me the whitethroat whistling in the hedge !

Why should I fret myself to find out nought ?
Dispute can blight the soul's eternal corn,
And choke its richness with the tares of thought.

I am content to know that God is great,
And Lord of fish and fowl, of air and sea—
Some little points are misty.   Let them wait

I well can wait when upland, wood and dell
Are full of speckled thrushes great with song,
And foxgloves chime each purple velvet bell.

Our village is encircled by sweet sound
Of bee and bird and lily-loving brook :
Hence, Unbelief, for this is holy ground !

At early dawn I stand upon the sod
And let the lark rain this upon my soul,—
The smaller in man's sight the nearer God.

At noon I linger by the curving stream,
And watch fresh water running to the sea
The salt of which comes not into its dream.

At eventide I lean across a gate,
And, knowing life must set as does the sun,
Muse on the angels in the happy state.

Nineteenth Century.

Ah, let me live among the birds and bloom
Of hazel copses and enchanted woods
Till death shall toll me to the common tomb.

Give me no coat of arms, no pomp, no pride,
But violets only and the rustic joys
That throne content along the country-side ;

No subtle readings, but a trusting love,
A hand to help, a heart to share in pain,
And over all the cooing of the dove.

How sweet the hedge that hides a cunning nest,
And curtains of a patient bright-eyed thrush
With five small worlds beneath her mottled
      breast !

Though life is growing nearer day by day
Each globe she loves as yet is mute, and still
Her bosom's beauty slowly wears away.

At last the thin blue veils are backward furled,
Existence wakes and pipes into a bird
As infant music bursts into the world.

And now the mother-thrush is proud and gay ;
She has her pretty cottage, and her young
To feed and lull when western skies turn grey.

It would be bitter work to set a snare,
Catch her and hang her in a London den
Unknown to sun and woodland wealth of air.

As with the thrush so would it be with me
If I should leave my red-tiled roof and push
My country shoulders through a living sea.

My song is all of birds and peasant homes,
For on such themes my heart delights to dwell
And sing in sunshine till the shadow comes.

I sing of daisies and the coloured plot
Where dandelions climb the thistle's knee—
I take what is, nor pine for what is not.

I am for finches and the rosy lass
Who leads me where the moss is thick, and where
Sweet strawberry-balls of scarlet gleam in grass.

And this I know, that when I leave my birds,
The lichened walls, the heartsease and the heath
I shall not wholly fail of kindly words.

And while I journey to the distant Day
That first shall dawn upon the eastern hills,
Perchance some thrush will sing me on my way.

The Great Republic lies towards the East,
And Daybreak comes when Christ with tender face
Welcomes the poor in spirit—who were least.

A MAID'S HOLIDAY

THE deep and silent undergrowth
    Shall be my home this summer day ;
The idle bird and breeze shall both
    Entrance me with their lay :

Nineteenth Century.

How cool to lie where shadows toss
  In revelry upon the turf,
And press my fingers in the moss,
  And be no more a serf!—

No more a slave to pen and ink;
  No more a slave to aching dread;
Released from cages where I think
  To win my daily bread.
O little blade of grass so soft,
  My heart is glad to find you here—
To find your slender lance aloft,
  With all your comrades near!

Is then your regiment, bright, alert
  In marching order, cooled by dew,
Camped here to watch that none may hurt
  The speedwell's speck of blue?
Or do you guard the foxglove-bloom
  That rings a chime it never tells,
Round which the bees in concert boom
  And rumble in its bells?

'Tis sweet indeed to lie and watch
  Faint figures in the open glades;
To see the pressing sweethearts snatch
  A tribute from the maids!
To hear the clink of milking-pails;
  The brisk and angry crack of whips
That startle Colin by the rails
  From touching Cicely's lips!

But best of all, with eyes devout,
  To gaze in silence at the sky,
And wonder if the dead look out
  Upon me as I lie:

Dainty Poems.

Across my patch of firmament
  So many angels seem to rove—
So many friends who died and went,
  Tho' not beyond my love !

I will not wrong their happiness,
  Nor lust to bring them back again,
For God will give fresh joys to ease
  The iron of my pain :
He sends me lilacs, pansies, pinks,
  This deep and silent undergrowth,
And sometimes, when my spirit sinks,
  The peace of utter sloth.

→§-§←

CUPID

Love, I met thee yesterday,
  With an empty quiver,
Coming from Clarinda's house
  By the reedy river.

And I saw Clarinda stand
  Near the pansies, weeping,
With her hands upon her breast,
  All thine arrows keeping.

When the dewdrops came like stars,
  Full of little flashes,
All Clarinda's tears I kissed
  From her shining lashes.

Richard le Gallienne

ORBITS

Two stars once on their lonely way
  Met in the heavenly height,
And they dreamed a dream they might shine
      alway
  With undivided light ;
Melt into one with a breathless throe,
  And beam as one in the night.

And each forgot in the dream so strange
  How desolately far
Swept on each path, for who shall change
  The orbit of a star ?
Yea, all was a dream, and they still must go
  As lonely as they are.

LOVE'S POOR

Yea, love, I know, and I would have it thus,
I know that not for us
Is springtide Passion with his fire and flowers,
I know this love of ours
Lives not, nor yet may live,
By the dear food that lips and hands can give.

Not, Love, that we in some high dream despise
The common lover's common Paradise ;
Ah, God, if Thou and I
But one short hour their blessedness might try,
How could we poor ones teach
Those happy ones who half forget them rich :
For if we thus endure,
'Tis only, love, because we are so poor.

A CHILD'S EVENSONG

THE sun is weary, for he ran
　So far and fast to-day ;
The birds are weary, for who sang
　So many songs as they ?
The bees and butterflies at last
　Are tired out, for just think too
How many gardens through the day
　Their little wings have fluttered through.
　And so, as all tired people do,
They've gone to lay their sleepy heads
Deep deep in warm and happy beds.
The sun has shut his golden eye
And gone to sleep beneath the sky,
The birds and butterflies and bees
Have all crept into flowers and trees,
And all lie quiet, still as mice,
Till morning comes—like father's voice.

So Geoffrey, Owen, Phyllis, you
Must sleep away till morning too.
Close little eyes, down little heads,
And sleep,—sleep—sleep in happy beds.

Nineteenth Century.

A POET hungered, as well he might—
Not a morsel since yesternight!
And sad he grew—good reason why—
For the poet had nought wherewith to buy.

"Are not two sparrows sold," he cried,
"Sold for a farthing?" and, he sighed,
As he pushed his morning post away,
"Are not two sonnets more than they?"

Yet store of gold, great store had he,—
Of the gold that is known as "faery."
He had the gold of his burning dreams,
He had his golden rhymes—in reams,
He had the strings of his golden lyre,
And his own was that golden west on fire.

But the poet knew his world too well
To dream that such would buy or sell.
He had his poets, "pure gold," he said,
But the man at the bookstall shook his head,
And offered a grudging half-a-crown
For the five the poet had brought him down.
Ah, what a world we are in! we sigh,
Where a lunch costs more than a Keats can buy,
And even Shakespeare's hallowed line
Falls short of the requisite sum to dine.

Yet other gold had the poet got,
For see from that grey-blue Gouda pot
Three golden tulips spouting flame—
From his love, from his love, this morn, they
    came

67

His love he loved even more than fame.
Three golden tulips thrice more fair
Than other golden tulips were—
" And yet," he smiled as he took one up,
And feasted on its yellow cup,—
" I wonder how many eggs you'd buy !
By Bacchus, I've half a mind to try !
One golden bloom, for one golden yolk—
Nay, on my word, sir, I mean no joke—
Gold for gold is fair dealing, sir."
Think of the grocer gaping there !

Or the baker, if I went and said,
" This tulip for a loaf of bread,
God's beauty for your kneaded grain ; "

Or the vintner—" For this flower of mine
A flagon, pray, of yellow wine,
And you shall keep the change for gain " ?

Ah me, on what a different earth
I and these fellows had our birth,
Strange that these golden things should be
For them so poor, so rich for me !

Ended his sigh, the poet searched his shelf—
Seeking another poet to feed himself ;
Then sadly went, and, full of shame and grief,
Sold his last Swinburne for a plate of beef !

Thus poets too, to fill the hungry maw,
Must eat each other—'tis the eternal law.

Nineteenth Century.

IN HER DIARY

Go, little book, and be the looking-glass
Of her dear soul,
The mirror of her moments as they pass,
Keeping the whole;
Wherein she still may look on yesterday
To-day to cheer,
And towards To-morrow pass upon her way
Without a fear.
For yesterday hath never won a crown,
However fair,
But that To-day a better for its own
Might win and wear;
And yesterday hath never joyed a joy,
However sweet,
That this To-day or that To-morrow too
May not repeat.
Think too, To-day is trustee for To-morrow,
And present pain
That's bravely borne shall ease the future
    sorrow;
Nor cry in vain.
"Spare us To-day, To-morrow bring the rod,'
For then again
To-morrow from to-morrow still shall borrow
A little ease to gain:
But bear to-day whate'er To-day may bring
'Tis the one way to make To-morrow sing.

Edmund Gosse

THE RETURN OF THE SWALLOWS

"Out in the meadows the young grass
    springs,
  Shivering with sap," said the larks, "and we
Shoot into air with our strong young wings,
  Spirally up over level and lea;
Come, O swallows, and fly with us
Now that horizons are luminous!
Evening and morning the world of light,
Spreading and kindling is infinite!"

Far away, by the sea in the south,
  The hills of olive and slopes of fern
Whiten and glow in the sun's long drouth,
  Under the heavens that beam and burn;
And all the swallows were gathered there
Flitting about in the fragrant air,
And heard no sound from the larks, but flew
Flashing under the blinding blue.

Out of the depths of their soft rich throats
  Languidly fluted the thrushes, and said:
"Musical thought in the mild air floats,
  Spring is coming and winter is dead!

Come, O swallows, and stir the air,
For the buds are all bursting unaware,
And the drooping eaves and the elm trees long
To hear the sound of your low sweet song."

Over the roofs of the white Algiers,
   Flashingly shadowing the bright bazaar,
Flitted the swallows, and not one hears
   The call of the thrushes from far, from far ;
Sighed the thrushes ; then, all at once,
Broke out singing the old sweet tones,
Singing the bridal of sap and shoot,
The tree's slow life between root and fruit.

But just when the dingles of April flowers
   Shine with the earliest daffodils,
When, before sunrise, the cold clear hours
   Gleam with a promise that noon fulfils,—
Deep in the leafage the cuckoo cried,
Perched on a spray by a rivulet side,
   Swallows, O swallows, come back again,
To swoop, and herald the April rain.

And something awoke in the slumbering heart
   Of the alien birds in their African air,
And they paused, and alighted, and twittered
     apart,
   And met in the broad white dreamy square,
And the sad slave woman, who lifted up
From the fountain her broad-lipped earthen
     cup,
Said to herself, with a weary sigh,
" To-morrow the swallows will northward fly ! "

Dainty Poems of the

TO T. H.

Between two golden tufts of summer grass,
I see the world through hot air as through glass,
And by my face sweet lights and colours pass.

Before me, dark against the fading sky,
I watch three mowers mowing, as I lie :
With brawny arms they sweep in harmony.

Brown English faces by the sun burnt red,
Rich glowing colour on bare throat and head,
My heart would leap to watch them, were I
    dead !

And in my strong young living as I lie,
I seem to move with them in harmony,—
A fourth is mowing, and the fourth am I.

The music of the scythes that glide and leap,
The young men whistling as their great arms
    sweep,
And all the perfume and sweet sense of sleep,

The weary butterflies that droop their wings,
The dreamy nightingale that hardly sings,
And all the lassitude of happy things,

Is mingling with the warm and pulsing blood
That gushes through my veins a languid flood
And feeds my spirit as the sap a bud.

Nineteenth Century.

Behind the mowers, on the amber air,
A dark-green beech-wood rises, still and fair,
A white path winding up it like a stair.

And see that girl, with pitcher on her head,
And clean white apron on her gown of red,—
Her even-song of love is but half-said :

She waits the youngest mower.   Now he goes ;
Her cheeks are redder than a wild blush-rose ;
They climb up where the deepest shadows close.

But though they pass and vanish, I am there ;
I watch his rough hands meet beneath her hair,
Their broken speech sounds sweet to me like
      prayer.

Ah ! now the rosy children come to play,
And romp and struggle with the new mown hay ;
Their clear high voices sound from far away.

They know so little why the world is sad,
They dig themselves warm graves and yet are
      glad ;
Their muffled screams and laughter make me
      mad !

I long to go and play among them there ;
Unseen, like wind, to take them by the hair,
And gently make their rosy cheeks more fair.

The happy children ! full of frank surprise,
And sudden whims and innocent ecstasies ;
What godhead sparkles from their liquid eyes !

No wonder round those urns of mingled clays
That Tuscan potters fashioned in old days,
And coloured like the torrid earth ablaze,

We find the little gods and loves portrayed,
Through ancient forests wandering undismayed,
And fluting hymns of pleasure unafraid.

They knew, as I do now, what keen delight
A strong man feels to watch the tender flight
Of little children playing in his sight.

I do not hunger for a well-stored mind,
I only wish to live my life, and find
My heart in unison with all mankind.

My life is like the single dewy star
That trembles on the horizon's primrose-bar,—
A microcosm where all things living are.

And if, among the noiseless grasses, Death
Should come behind and take away my breath,
I should not rise as one who sorroweth ;

For I should pass, but all the world would be
Full of desire and young delight and glee,
And why should men be sad through loss of me ?

The light is flying ; in the silver-blue
The young moon shines from her bright win-
    dow through :
The mowers are all gone, and I go too.

+8·34+

Nineteenth Century.

SERENADE

The lemon-petals gently fall
    Within the windless Indian night,
The wild liana'd waterfall
    Hangs, lingering like a ghostly light;
Drop down to me, and linger long, my heart's
        entire delight.

Among the trees, the fiery flies
    Move slowly in their robes of flame;
Above them, through the liquid skies,
    The stars in squadrons do the same;
Move through the garden down to me, and
        softly speak my name!

By midnight's moving heart that shakes
    The coloured air and kindling gloom,
By all the forms that beauty takes
    In fruit, in blossom, in perfume,
Come down and still the aching doubts that
        haunt me and consume!

Else if the chilly morning break
    And thou hast heard my voice in vain,
Unmoved as is a forest-lake
    That through the branches hears the rain,
Beware lest Love himself pass by to bless thee,
        and—refrain!

75

MOORLAND

Now the buttercups of May
Twinkle fainter day by day,
    And the stalks of flowering clover
    Make the June fields red all over,—

Now the cuckoo, like a bell,
Modulates a sad farewell,
    And the nightingale, perceiving
    Love's warm tokens, ends her grieving,—

Let us twain arise and go
Where the freshening breezes blow,
    Where the granite giant moulders
    In his circling cairn of boulders !

Just a year ago to-day,
Friend, we climbed the self-same way,
    Through the village-green, and higher,
    Past the smithy's thundering fire ;

Up and up and where the hill
Wound us by the cider-still ;
    Where the scythers from the meadow
    Sat along the hedge for shadow ;

Where the little wayside inn
Signals that the moors begin,
    Ah ! remember all our laughter,
    Loitering at the bar,—and after !

All must be the same to-day,
All must look the same old way,
    Only that the sweet child-maiden
    We admired so well, fruit-laden,

Nineteenth Century.

Now, like an expanded bud,
Must be blown to womanhood,
   And the fuller lips and bosom
   Must proclaim the perfect blossom.

One step more ! Before us, lo !
Sheer the great ravine below,
   Empty, save where one brown plover
   Wheels across the ferny cover !

Here, where all the valley lies
Like a scroll before our eyes,
   Let us spend our golden leisure
   In a world of lazy pleasure ;

Comrade, let your heart forget
All the thoughts that fray and fret ;
   Till the sun-down flares out yonder,
   Stretch here in the fern, and ponder.

See, below us, where the stream
Winds with broken silver gleam,
   How the nervous quivering sallows
   Bend and dare not touch the shallows.

In that willow-shaded pool,
When last June the airs were cool,
   How we made the hot noon shiver
   With our plunge into the river.

In the sweet sun, side by side
You and I and none beside !
   Head and hands, thrown backward, slacken,
   Sunk into the soft warm bracken.

Up in heaven a milky sky
Floats across us leisurely ;
   When we close our eyes, the duller
   Half-light seems a faint red colour.

In this weary life of ours
Pass too many leaden hours ;
   In our chronicles of passion
   Too much apes the world's dull fashion.

If our spirits strive to be
Pure and high in their degree,
   Let us learn the soaring pæan
   Under God's own empyrean.

Leisure in the sun and air
Makes the spirit strong and fair ;
   Flaccid veins and pallid features
   Are not fit for sky-born creatures.

Come then, for the hours of May
Wane and falter, day by day,
   And the thrushes' first June chorus
   Will have walked the woods before us !

—>6-3<—

SUNSHINE BEFORE SUNRISE

THE ice-white mountains clustered all around
    us,
   But arctic summer blossomed at our feet ;
The perfume of the creeping sallows found us,
   The cranberry-flowers were sweet.

Nineteenth Century.

The reindeer champed the ghostly moss, and
        over
    The sparkling peat that crowned the dim
        ravine
The sky was violet-blue; and loved by lover
    We clung, and lay half-seen.

Below us through the valley crept a river,
    Cleft round an island where the Lap-men lay;
Its sluggish water dragged with slow endeavour
    The mountain-snows away.

One thin blue curl of wood-smoke rose up
        single,—
    The only sign of life the valley gave;
But where the fern-roots and the streamlets
        mingle
    Our hearts were warm and brave.

My arm was round her small head sweetly
        fashioned,
    Her bright head shapely as a hyacinth bell;
So silent were we that our hearts' impassioned
    Twin-throb was audible.

Alas! for neither knew the language spoken
    Amongst the people whence the other came;
A few brief words were all we had for token,
    And just each other's name.

" *My love is pure as this blue heaven above you,*"
    I said,—but saw she let the meaning slip;
" Jeg elsker Dem," I felt must be " I love you!"
    And answered, lip to lip.

Oh ! how the tender throbbing of her bosom
  Beat bird-like, crushed to mine in that em-
      brace;
While blushes, like the light through some red
      blossom,
  Dyed all her dewy face.

There is no night-time in the northern summer,
  But golden shimmer fills the hours of sleep,
And sunset fades not, till the bright new-comer,
  Red sunrise, smites the deep.

But when the blue snow-shadows grew intenser
  Across the peaks against the golden sky,
And on the hills the knots of deer grew denser,
  And raised their tender cry,

And wandered down to the Lap-men's dwelling,
  We knew our long sweet day was nearly spent,
And slowly, with our hearts within us swelling,
  Our homeward steps we bent.

Down rugged paths and torrents mad with
      foaming,
  With clinging hands, we loitered, blind with
      joy,
I thought a long life spent like this in roaming
  Would never tire or cloy.

And very late we saw before us, dreaming,
  The red-roofed town where all her days had
      been,
And far beyond, half shaded and half gleaming,
  The blue sea, flecked with green.

Nineteenth Century.

Ah! sweet is life and sweet is youth's young
    passion,
  And sweet the first kiss on a girl's warm
    cheek ;
Since then we both have learnt in broken fashion
  Each other's tongue to speak ;

And many days and nights of love and pleasure
  Have laid their fragrant chaplets on our hair,
And many hours of eloquent wise leisure
  Have made our lives seem fair ;

But Memory knows not where so white a
    place is
  In all her shining catalogue of hours,
As that one day of silent warm embraces
  Among the cranberry-flowers.

Eugene Lee-Hamilton

AN ELFIN SKATE

1.

THEY wheeled me up the snow-cleared garden
    way,
And left me where the dazzling heaps were
    thrown ;
And as I mused on winter sports once known,
Up came a tiny man to where I lay.

He was six inches high ; his beard was gray
As silver frost ; his coat and cap were brown,
Of mouse's fur ; while two wee skates hung
    down
From his wee belt, and gleamed in winter's ray.

He clambered up my couch, and eyed me long.
" Show me thy skates," said I ; " for once, alas !
I, too, could skate. What pixie mayst thou
    be ? "

" I am the King," he answered, " of the throng
Called Winter Elves. We live in roots, and
    pass
The summer months in sleep. Frost sets us
    free."

Dainty Poems.

II.

" We find by moonlight little pools of ice,
Just one yard wide," the imp of winter said ;
" And skate all night, while mortals are in bed,
In tiny circles of our Elf device ;

And when it snows we harness forest mice
To wee bark sleighs, with lightest fibrous thread,
And scour the woods ; or play all night instead
With snowballs large as peas, well patted thrice.

But is it true, as I have heard them say,
That thou canst share in winter games no more,
But liest motionless year in year out ?

That must be hard.   To-day I cannot stay,
But I'll return each year, when all is hoar,
And tell thee when the skaters are about."

III.

On my wheeled bed, I let my fingers play
With a wee silver skate, scarce one inch long,
Which might have fitted one of Frost's Elf
        throng,
Or been his gift to one whose limbs are clay.

But Elfdom's dead ; and what in my hand lay
Was out of an old desk, from years, when
        strong
And full of health, life sang me still its song ;
A skating club's small badge, long stowed away.

Oh, there is nothing like the skater's art—
The poetry of circles; nothing like
The fleeting beauty of his crystal floor.

Above his head the winter sunbeams dart;
Beneath his feet flits past the frightened pike.
Skate while you may; the morrow skates no
    more.

—>¦¦<—

ON A SURF-ROLLED TORSO OF VENUS

(*Discovered at Tripoli Vecchio*)

ONE day, in the world's youth, long, long
    ago,
Before the golden hair of Time grew gray,
The bright warm sea, scarce stirred by dolphin's
    play,
Was swept by sudden music strange and low;

And rippling with the kisses zephyrs blow,
Gave forth a dripping goddess, whose strong
    sway
All earth, all air, all wave was to obey,
Throned on a shell more rosy than dawn's glow.

And, lo, that self-same sea has now upthrown
A mutilated Venus, roll'd, and roll'd
For centuries in surf, and who has grown

More soft, more chaste, more lovely than of old,
With every line made vague, so that the stone
Seems seen as through a veil which Ages hold.

Nineteenth Century.

Now is the time when Nature may display
Her frosty jewelry in all men's eyes,
And every breeze that through the brushwood
    sighs
Brings down her brilliants in a glittering spray.

Like drops of blood upon the snow-strewn way,
The crimson berries lie, the robins' prize ;
While, in the leafless woods, the poor man tries
To find some faggots for the bitter day.

On every sleeping pool the winter fits
With unseen hand a strong and glassy lid ;
The frightened fish beneath the skater flits,

And quaking, in the lowest depths lies hid ;
And old King Christmas at his revel sits,
Where all whom hunger pinches not are bid.

SPRING

There lurks a sadness in the April air
For those who note the fate of early things,
A dreamy sense of what the future brings
To those too good, too hopeful or too fair.

An underthought of heartache, as it were,
Blends with the pæan that the new leaf sings ;
And, as it were, a breeze from Death's great
    wings
Shakes down the blossoms that the fruit-trees
    bear.

The tide of sap flows up the forest trees ;
The birds exult in every bough on high ;
The ivy bloom is full of humming bees ;

But if you list, you hear the latent sigh ;
And each new leaf that rustles in the breeze
Proclaims the boundless mutability.

—⸾⸾⸾—

OBERON'S LAST COUNCIL

I.

IF, on some woodland lawn, you see a ring
Of darker hue upon the paler grass—
The strange green growth which children as
    they pass
Still tell each other is a fairy thing

Left by the Elves o'er-night—let your soul cling
To the sweet thought that there the Elf King
    was
With all his crew at dawn ; but that, alas !
They met there for their last, last gathering.

Nineteenth Century.

For they are fled : and though the sunshine still
Dances in flecks, as dance the leaves above,
And still the squirrel nibbles and the mouse,

The little folk are gone who used to fill
The hazel copses where the wild wood-dove
With cross-laid twigs still builds her breezy
    house.

II.

He called a last assembly of the Elves.
Hundreds of Fairies in the forest met
Round one huge oak-tree—Sprites of dry and
    wet,
Pixies and Imps, and every Gnome that delves:

And Oberon said: "We lurk by tens and
    twelves,
Starved in the woods.   Man's faith—our food
    as yet—
Feeds us no more ; the Fairies' sun has set :
We are but shadows of our former selves.

'Tis time to leave the woods and we must part.
When faith quite ends—so say the High
    Decrees—
Then death will strike us with his icy dart.

Long have we nestled in the hearts of trees ;
Now we must nestle in the Poet's heart—
The only place where fairies never freeze."

—➤-&-3-⤙-

THE DEATH OF PUCK

I.

I FEAR that Puck is dead—it is so long
Since men last saw him—dead with all the rest
Of that sweet Elfin crew that made their nest
In hollow huts, where hazels sing their song;

Dead and for ever, like the antique throng
The Elves replaced; the Dryad that you guessed
Behind the leaves; the Naiad weed-bedressed;
The leaf-eared Faun that loved to lead you
    wrong.

Tell me, thou hopping Robin, hast thou met
A little man, no bigger than thyself,
Whom they call Puck, where woodland bells
    are wet?

Tell me, thou Wood-mouse, hast thou seen an
    Elf
Whom they call Puck, and is he seated yet,
Capped with a snail-shell, on his mushroom
    shelf?

II.

The Robin gave three hops, and chirped, and
    said:
"Yes, I knew Puck, and loved him; though I
    trow
He mimicked oft my whistle, chuckling low;
Yes, I knew cousin Puck; but he is dead.

Nineteenth Century.

We found him lying on his mushroom bed—
The Wren and I—half covered up with snow,
As we were hopping where the berries grow.
We think he died of cold.   Ay, Puck is fled."

And then the Wood-mouse said: "We made
    the Mole
Dig him a little grave beneath the moss,
And four big Dormice placed him in the hole.

The Squirrel made with sticks a little cross ;
Puck was a Christian Elf, and had a soul ;
And all we velvet jackets mourn his loss."

—►§-§◄—

JAMES WATT TO THE SPIRIT OF HIS KETTLE
1765

I SIT beside the hearth, and, for an hour,
I watch the steam that shakes the kettle's lid,
Like some live thing that struggles hard to rid
Its limbs of bondage, and assert its power.

Yea, like some fiend that Solomon made cower,
And, who for countless centuries was bid
Dwell in a bottle which the deep sea hid,
Where, tight compressed, it panted still to
    tower ;

What if this vapour were a stronger thing
Than all the genii cast into the sea
And curst forever by the Wizard King?

And what if I one day should set it free,
And break the seal of Solomon's own ring,
And make the Dæmon do my drudgery?

LADY JANE GREY TO THE FLOWERS AND BIRDS
1553

To-MORROW death: and there are woods
    hard by,
With restless spots of sunshine on the ground,
With bees that hum and birds that pipe all round,
And beds of moss where sparkling dewdrops
    lie ;

To-morrow death : and there are fields of rye
Where poppies and bright corn-flowers abound ;
And there are fragrant grasses, where the sound
Of streamlets rises, where the mowers ply.

I wonder if the woodland bells will close
A little earlier on the day I end,
Tired of the light, though free from human
    woes ;

And if the Robin and the Thrush will wend
A little sooner to their sweet repose,
To make a little mourning for their friend?

Nineteenth Century.

HANNIBAL PETRONI TO CLAUDIA MALASPADA
1559

I WOULD that all the sparkling stones that find
Their way to Philip's treasury were mine ;
And all the Pearls that nations pay in fine
To some victorious soldan of far Ind.

That I might strew the garden paths that wind
Beneath thy casement with all gems that shine,
Fit gravel for no other feet but thine
This summer night, thou shadow on the blind!

Gems have I none.   But see, from Heaven's hem
The moon is strewing opals for thy feet,
And turns each vulgar pebble to a gem ;

Come forth, come forth: the night is warm
        and sweet,
Each flower sleeps upon its silvered stem,
And all is hushed, save our two hearts that beat.

—➤⟞⟝⟞3⟝⟝—

ARABELLA STUART TO THE UNSEEN SPRING
1612

IT must be Spring ; a long bright slanting ray
Peeps daily in and warms my prison now ;
While, through the bars, on which I rest my
        brow,
A twittering of swallows finds its way.

The world must now be full of thorny may ;
Bright speckled butterflies ; young leaves that
    glow ;
Ripe fragrant grass ; fresh banks where wild
    bells grow ;
Bleatings and whistlings ; cuckoo notes all day.

Thou peeping ray of Spring, go kiss the corn
That sprouts beneath the breeze, and never pry
Into this cell, where Misery pines forlorn ;

Ye happy, happy swallows, that can fly
On Spring's own breath, oh, twitter not such
    scorn
Of earth, and woe, and of captivity !

—>&-3<—

ISAAC WALTON TO RIVER AND BROOK
1650

WHICH is more sweet,—the slow mysterious
    stream,
Where sleeps the pike throughout the long
    noon hours,
Which moats with emerald old Cathedral towers,
And winds through tufted timber like the dream

That glides through summer sleep ; where
    white swans teem,
And dragon flies and broad-leaved floating
    flowers,
Where through the hanging boughs you see the
    mowers
Among the grasses, whet their scythes that
    gleam ;

Or that blue brook where leaps the speckled
    trout,
That laughs and sings and dances on its way
Among a thousand bafflings in and out ;

Bubbling and gurgling through the livelong day
Between the stones, in riot, reel and rout,
While rays of sun make rainbows in the spray ?

SIR WALTER RALEIGH TO A CAGED LINNET
1608

Thou tiny solace of these prison days,
Too long already have I kept thee here ;
With every week thou hast become more dear—
So dear that I will free thee : fly thy way.

Man, the alternate slave and tyrant, lays
Too soon on others what he has to bear.
Thy cage is in my cage ; but, never fear,
The sun once more shall bathe thee with its rays.

Fly forth, and tell the sunny woods how oft
I think of them, and stretch my limbs in thought
Upon their fragrant mosses green and soft ;

And whistle all the whistlings God hath taught
Thy throat, to other songsters high aloft—
Not to a captive who can answer nought.

Bret Harte

A NEWPORT ROMANCE.

THEY say that she died of a broken heart
  (I tell the tale as 'twas told to me);
But her spirit lives, and her soul is part
  Of this sad old house by the sea.

Her lover was fickle and fine and French:
  It was nearly a hundred years ago
When he sailed away from her arms—poor
    wench !—
  With the Admiral Rochambeau.

I marvel much what periwigged phrase
  Won the heart of this sentimental Quaker,
At what golden-laced speech of those modish
    days
  She listened—the mischief take her !

But she kept the posies of mignonette
  That he gave ; and ever as their bloom failed
And faded (though with her tears still wet),
  Her youth with their own exhaled.

Till one night, when the sea-fog wrapped a shroud
  Round spar and spire and tarn and tree,
Her soul went upon that lifted cloud
  From this sad old house by the sea.

Dainty Poems.

And ever since then when the clock strikes two,
  She walks unbidden from room to room,
And the air is filled that she passes through
  With a subtle, sad perfume.

The delicate odour of mignonette,
  The ghost of a dead and gone bouquet,
Is all that tells of her story ; yet,
  Could she think of a sweeter way?

    •   •   •   •   •   •   •   •

I sit in the sad old house to-night,—
  Myself a ghost from a farther sea ;
And I trust that this Quaker woman might,
  In courtesy, visit me.

For the laugh is fled from porch and lawn,
  And the bugle died from the fort on the hill,
And the twitter of girls on the stairs is gone,
  And the grand piano is still.

Somewhere in the darkness a clock strikes two ;
  And there is no sound in the sad old house,
But the long veranda dripping with dew,
  And in the wainscot a mouse.

The light of my study lamp streams out
  From the library door, but has gone astray
In the depths of the darkened hall. Small
    doubt
  But the Quakeress knows the way.

Was it the trick of a sense o'erwrought
  With outward watching and inward fret?
But I swear that the air just now was fraught
  With the odour of mignonette !

I open the window, and seem almost —
    So still lies the ocean—to hear the beat
Of its Great Gulf artery off the Coast,
    And to bask in its tropic heat.

In my neighbour's windows the gas-lights flare,
    As the dancers swing in a waltz of Strauss;
And I wonder now could I fit that air
    To the song of this sad old house.

And no odour of mignonette there is
    But the breath of morn on the dewy lawn;
And mayhap from causes as slight as this
    The quaint old legend is born.

But the soul of that subtle, sad perfume,
    As the spiced embalmings they say outlast
The mummy laid in his rocky tomb,
    Awakens my buried past.

And I think of the passion that shook my youth,
    Of its aimless loves and its idle pains,
And am thankful now for the certain truth
    That only the sweet remains.

And I hear no rustle of stiff brocade,
    And I see no face at my library door;
For now that the ghosts of my heart are laid,
    She is viewless for evermore.

But whether she came as a faint perfume,
    Or whether a spirit in stole of white,
I feel, as I pass from the darkened room,
    She has been with my soul to-night!

WHAT THE CHIMNEY SANG

Over the chimney the night wind sang,
And chanted a melody no one knew :
And the woman stopped, and her babe she
  tossed,
And thought of the one she had long since lost,
And said as her tear-drops back she forced,
" I hate the wind in the chimney."

Over the chimney the night wind sang,
And chanted a melody no one knew ;
And the children said, as they closer drew,
" 'Tis some witch that is cleaving the black
  night through,
'Tis a fairy trumpet that just then blew,
And we fear the wind in the chimney."

Over the chimney the night wind sang,
And chanted a melody no one knew ;
And the man, as he sat on his hearth below,
Said to himself, " It will surely snow,
And fuel is dear and wages low,
And I'll stop the leak in the chimney."

Over the chimney the night wind sang,
And chanted a melody no one knew ;
But the poet listened and smiled, for he
Was man, and woman, and child, all three,
And said, " It is God's own harmony,
This wind we hear in the chimney."

➤⧈⧏

DICKENS IN CAMP

Above the pines the moon was slowly drifting,
    The river sang below ;
The dim Sierras, far beyond, uplifting
    Their minarets of snow.

The roaring camp-fire, with rude humour, painted
    The ruddy tints of health
On haggard face and form that drooped and fainted
    In the fierce race for wealth ;

Till one arose, and from his pack's scant treasure
    A hoarded volume drew,
And cards were dropped from hands of listless leisure
    To hear the tale anew.

And then, while round them shadows gathered faster,
    And as the firelight fell,
He read aloud the book wherein the Master
    Had writ of " Little Nell."

Perhaps 'twas boyish fancy,—for the reader
    Was youngest of them all,—
But, as he read, from clustering pine and cedar
    A silence seemed to fall ;

The fir-trees, gathering closer in the shadows,
    Listened in every spray,
While the whole camp, with " Nell" on English meadows
    Wandered and lost their way.

And so in mountain solitudes—o'ertaken
    As by some spell divine—
Their cares dropped from them like the needles
    shaken
    From out the gusty pine.

Lost is that camp and wasted all its fire :
    And he who wrought that spell?—
Ah! towering pine and stately Kentish spire,
    Ye have one tale to tell!

Lost is that camp, but let its fragrant story
    Blend with the breath that thrills
With hop-vine's incense all the pensive glory
    That fills the Kentish hills.

And on that grave where English oak and holly
    And laurel wreaths entwine,
Deem it not all a too presumptuous folly,—
    This spray of Western pine!

—>&-3<—

RELIEVING GUARD

T. S. K. *Obiit March 4, 1864.*

CAME the relief. "What, Sentry, ho!
  How passed the night through thy long
    waking?"
"Cold, cheerless, dark,—as may befit
  The hour before the dawn is breaking."

"No sight? no sound?" "No; nothing save
  The plover from the marches calling,
And in yon western sky, about
  An hour ago, a star was falling."

"A star? There's nothing strange in that."
  "No, nothing; but, above the thicket
Somehow it seemed to me that God
  Somewhere had just relieved a picket."

FATE

"THE sky is clouded, the rocks are bare,
The spray of the tempest is white in air,
The winds are out with the waves at play,
And I shall not tempt the sea to-day.

"The trail is narrow, the wood is dim,
The panther clings to the arching limb,
And the lion's whelps are abroad at play,
And I shall not join in the chase to-day."

But the ship sailed safely over the sea,
And the hunters came home from the chase in
      glee,
And the town that was builded upon a rock
Was swallowed up in the earthquake shock.

Nineteenth Century.

ON THE LANDING

(An Idyl of the Balusters)

BOBBY, ætat. 3½.   JOHNNY, ætat. 4½.

BOBBY.

Do you know why they've put us in that back-
  room,
  Up in the attic, close against the sky,
And made believe our nursery's a cloak-room?
      Do you know why?

JOHNNY.

No more I don't, nor why that Sammy's mother,
  What Ma thinks horrid, 'cause he bunged my
  eye,
Eats an ice cream, down there, like any other—
      No more don't I !

BOBBY.

Do you know why nurse says it isn't manners
  For you and me to ask folks twice for pie,
And no one hits that man with two bananas?
      Do you know why?

JOHNNY.

No more I don't, nor why that girl, whose
  dress is
  Off of her shoulders, don't catch cold and
  die,
When you and me gets croup when we un-
  dresses !
      No more don't I !

BOBBY

Perhaps she ain't as good as you and I is,
   And God don't want her up there in the sky,
And lets her live—to come in just when pie is—
        Perhaps that's why?

JOHNNY.

Do you know why that man that's got a
    cropped head
Rubbed it just now as if he felt a fly?
Could it be, Bobby, something that I dropded?
        And is that why?

BOBBY.

Good boys behaves, and so they don't get
    scolded,
   Nor drop hot milk on folks as they pass by.

JOHNNY. (*piously*).

Marbles would bounce on Mr Jones' bald head—
      But *I* shan't try!

BOBBY.

Do you know why Aunt Jane is always snarling
   At you and me because we tells a lie,
And she don't slap that man that called her
    darling?
      Do you know why?

JOHNNY.

No more I don't, nor why that man with
    Mamma
Just kissed her hand.

BOBBY.

> She hurt it—and that's why,
> He made it well, the very way that Mamma
> Does do to I.

JOHNNY.

> I feel so sleepy. . . . Was that Papa kissed
> us?
> What made him sigh, and look up to the sky?

BOBBY.

> We wer'n't downstairs, and he and God had
> missed us,
> And that was why!

John Hay

A WOMAN'S LOVE

A SENTINEL angel sitting high in glory
Heard this shrill wail ring out from Purgatory:
"Have mercy, mighty angel, hear my story!

"I loved,—and, blind with passionate love, I
    fell.
Love brought me down to death, and death to
    Hell.
For God is just, and death for sin is well.

"I do not rage against his high decree,
Nor for myself do ask that grace shall be;
But for my love on earth who mourns for me.

"Great Spirit! Let me see my love again
And comfort him one hour, and I were fain
To pay a thousand years of fire and pain."

Then said the pitying angel, "Nay, repent
That wild vow! Look, the dial-finger's bent
Down to the last hour of thy punishment!"

But still she wailed, "I pray thee, let me go!
I cannot rise to peace and leave him so.
O, let me soothe him in his bitter woe!"

Dainty Poems.

The brazen gates ground sullenly ajar,
And upward, joyous, like a rising star,
She rose and vanished in the ether far.

But soon adown the dying sunset sailing,
And like a wounded bird her pinions trailing,
She fluttered back, with broken-hearted wailing.

She sobbed, "I found him by the summer sea
Reclined, his head upon a maiden's knee,—
She curled his hair and kissed him. Woe is me!"

She wept, "Now let my punishment begin!
I have been fond and foolish. Let me in
To expiate my sorrow and my sin."

The angel answered, "Nay, sad soul, go higher!
To be deceived in your true heart's desire
Was bitterer than a thousand years of fire!"

DISTICHS

I.

Wisely a woman prefers to a lover a man
   who neglects her.
This one may love her some day, some day the
   lover will not.

II.

There are three species of creatures who when
   they seem coming are going,
When they seem going they come : Diplomates,
   women, and crabs.

Dainty Poems.

III.

Pleasures too hastily tasted grow sweeter in
    fond recollection,
As the pomegranate plucked green ripens far
    over the sea.

IV.

As the meek beasts in the Garden came flock-
    ing for Adam to name them,
Men for a title to-day crawl to the feet of a
    king.

V.

What is a first love worth, except to prepare for
    a second ?
What does the second love bring ? Only re-
    gret for the first.

VI.

Health was wooed by the Romans in groves of
    the laurel and myrtle.
Happy and long are the lives brightened by
    glory and love.

Alfred Hayes

THE MARCH OF MAN

Blind—then a little light—and once more
  blind.
Blind in birth's living shroud, there blindly
  reared,
Thence blindly driven—and lo ! a drowsy babe,
Its red face wrinkled like a fresh-blown poppy,
Whose silken petals keep awhile the crease
Of every fold they slept in.   Day by day
The light grows friendlier, till the strange great
  eyes,
So vastly vacant, so profoundly grave,
Stare hopeless, fearless, loveless at the world.
Then dawn of soul and day of strength, then
  dusk
Of fading dreams—a sigh—and once more
  blind.

From darkness unto darkness ; and this hour
Of shattered lanterns and of naked lights
Doth but the more reveal the enfolding gloom.
What recked our brute forefathers of the cave ?
They slew and ate, begat and slept ; to them
Earth seemed not one stale cradle, one stale
  tomb,

Floating untended through the boundless void ;
The weakling's moan, the spoil of lust and rage
To them brought no misgivings ; and we saints,
We sinners, curbed and bridled into crime,
Our tender souls self-tortured with remorse,
Envy them oft their blameless guiltiness.

Death grins at birth and birth makes mock of
    death ;
Death, birth, and death—O weary, weary round,
If self were all !—to think it, is to droop,
To live it, is to die.   Away with self !
Not beasts of prey, but human hearts of love !
Not claws of greed, but eager hands of help !
Not civil foes, but comrades in one cause !
Forward ! we cannot backward, if we would—
Forward through law to righteous lawlessness !

The generations pass into the dark ;
They fold themselves in silence, and are gone ;
Their loves and hates, ambitions, wrongs and
    tears,
Pangs of the body, puzzles of the brain,
Vex them no more.   In vain our men of light
Dissect the living nerve, in vain our priests
Plead with the God of old, in vain our seers
Question the heart of mystery—the deep
Gives back no answer, and the ghosts that
    thronged
Faith's morning-twilight visit not her noon.

Noon ?—rides the sun so high ?—or lingers low
Beyond the horizon, while we wisely take

Nineteenth Century.

Marsh-lights for stars, and starlight for the
 prime?
Those altars yet outface the storm, whereby
The gaunt white-bearded prophet of our sires
Stood, drenched with human gore; he doubted
 not
His night was day; and we, who hail some few
Pale streaks of morning, howsoever fair
And fraught with promise, for the light of
 noon—
That open glory of the sunlight heavens,
That desert-dreamland moving as we move—
Are blind as he, and children of his pride.

   .   .   .   .   .

                    What remains
To hope and toil for?—Fear not; heights be-
 yond
Our short horizon then will tower afar,
Tempting to effort; scarcely hath man spelt
Through nature's alphabet, whose magic book
Holds in each word a universe; scarce kissed
The hem of art's rich robe, and scarce explored
A single creek of music's welling stream,
That whispers now along the reeds, now laughs
O'er pebbly beds, now roars below the rocks,
And lastly flows, a broad majestic flood,
Bearing the souls of millions with its tide,
Into the main of song.—'Tis much, that now,
Even in these murky days of greed and want,
Beauty hath smiled and wisdom turned her
 lamp
On thousands, where till late all things were
 dark.

Tis somewhat—and the commune of such souls
Is life's best boon ;—but when the promised sun
Hath risen, and equal laws and manners shed
Their genial influence o'er the minds of men,
Growths sweet and strange shall flourish,
    blossomings
Undreamt-of deck the highways hateful now
With tumult, dust and blood ; and human
    souls
Shall know an intercourse more wide and free,
More lofty, true and delicate, than aught
Our dullness can imagine ; genius then
Shall burst its chains ; no longer shall bare
    want
Turn men to beasts, the sordid strife for gain
Shrivel and starve the soul, nor idle riches
Gorge it to slumber ; Fortune's foolish sons
Shall lift no more a languid brow of scorn,
Nor lackeys do them worship ; but each man
Shall move amidst his peers, and frankly meet
His neighbour's gaze, and find him, not as now
In guise and bearing, thought, desire and speech
An alien, but a fellow.   Fancy then
Shall browse at large, wisdom enrich her store
Ten thousandfold ; art, like the gladsome sun
Revealing, through the gray, heaven's bound-
    less blue
And earth's fair shapes and tints, shall mount
    her throne,
Scatter night's sullen clouds, and light the
    world ;
And music, like the common flood of life,
Well in the hearts of all men.

.   .   .   .   .

Nineteenth Century.

Then not the chance of birth,
Nor hoarded gold wrung from the weak and
    poor,
But only the true kinghood of high souls,
The hero's glory, and the godlike brow
Of genius, shall have worship ; then shall glad-
    ness
Course through the people's veins as when the
    hearts
Of some vast throng are thrilling to one strain
Of lofty music ; pleasure shall not need
To hide her eyes, ashamed that others' grief
Pays for her pastime ; luxury's sick craving,
That owns no bound and therefore owns no
    peace,
That feeding but provoketh, shall be turned
To wholesome hunger, and lust's lawlessness
To wise and sweet restraint ; and Earth's best
    boon,
The fellowship of hand and head and heart,
The commune of true souls, shall lighten toil
And heal life's deep divisions.

                But such boon
Will never bless mankind till the dark gulf
'Twixt rich and poor, 'twixt sage and fool,
    'twixt churl
And gentle is bridged over—for true friends
Are ever equals ;—and that golden field,
That gladsome harvest of man's fellowship,
Now springing round our feet, will only reach
Its fulness after sunlight of free thought
And sun-warmth of wide sympathy have nursed
Its growth for ages.

    •   •   •   •   •   •   •   •

A mighty change,
Enfolded in the troubled womb of time,
Shapeth itself in silence ; foolish hopes
And fond alarms disquiet faithless breasts ;
Love waits the birth unfaltering.—The wise
    world
Hath not forgot how in a simple room
A Jewish craftsman with his fisher-friends
Once ate their farewell supper ; high priests
    hissed
Their spite ; Rome curled a lip of sickly scorn ;
But life was with the little brother-band,
And mankind's slow salvation.—Love can wait.

WITH FLOWERS

If these smile bright, believe they know
    That beauty is a flower ;
If crushed and drooping, they confess
    Thy smile's victorious power ;
If they look pale, it is because
    They pined and paled for thee ;
And if they blush, believe their hearts
    Are trembling consciously.
They wither, doomed through death alone
    To greet a flower more fair ;
Yet, ere they perish, kiss them once,
    'Twill raise thine image there ;
For often as thy fragrant breath
    Is mingling with their scents,
There meet an angel and a flower,
    Thine own pure elements.

Nineteenth Century.

CRASH out, ye mighty chords!—The heavens
    are black
With wrath; the lightnings shudder through
    the air,
    And blind with fury tear
        The huddling rack,
Furling its pale and tattered banners o'er
        Yon steel expanse;
Tender as new-born love a rainbow glows,
The warm mist 'neath it flushes moist and rose,
    City and sea and shore
        Steeped in one trance.

And every tree-top sparkles with its leaves
    Refulgent in the setting sun;
The meads are golden-green, rich with the storm
        Of Nature's summer-love;
        Far in the night above
A white bird twinkles like a star, and cleaves
        The thunder-caverns dun;
Denser and louder forth the sullen tempests
    swarm.

Crash out, vast symphony!—thy lover hears
And worships.—It is over—those fierce tears
    Have blotted all to grey;
        With smothered moan
Great nature's passion-music, like our own,
        Is sobbed away.

AUTUMN SONG

THE year grows heavy ; but the hour
Is fresh as April ; the blithe air
Is tremulous with sun and shower ;
   A rainbow smiles farewell
To the spent storm, and everywhere
   Song breaks from hill and dell.

So when the summer of our life
Fades into autumn, now and then
An hour will come to us, sweet wife,
   When all our soul shall sing,
And all our heart shall leap, as when
   We drank the dew of spring.

SERENADE

WHEN moonlight o'er thy casement weaves
Its network through the breathless leaves,
And lake and lawn beneath the summer sky
     Dream in the mist—
Ah ! sweet ! a lovelier scene within doth lie
     By slumber kist.

And when the stars begin to pale,
And trampling on her crimson veil
Young Morning flashes forth with dewy hair
     And sparkling eyes—
Ah ! sweet ! I linger for a dawn more fair;
     When thou shalt rise.

Nineteenth Century.

TO SWEET SEVENTEEN

To thee, young queen, these tribute lines,
  Charged with my love—the word is writ
A daintier word were false ; but "love"
  No more can tell the soul of it,

Than "light" can tell the myriad mood
  Of sunshine : from the fickle play
Which frolics through the dappled leaves
  When all the lanes are white with May,

To that full bliss of warmth which lies
  Delirious on the breast of June,
Or sunset flash of burdened heavens,
  Or dreamy glow of autumn noon.

So "love"—poor word—is all we have,
  To paint each radiant power that makes
The sunshine of a human heart ;
  From the sweet sense of want which wakes

In childhood's breast, to ripe repose
  Of wedded faith or ecstasy
Of passionate youth, or such delight
  As that I take, fair girl, in thee.

LIGHT AND LOVE

Front not the sun ; or, dazzled by his white-
      ness
Earth's face will seem expressionless and dim,
Features confused and beauty drowned in
      brightness ;
          But turn from him,

And thou wilt find familiar scenes and homely
Transfigured with a tender atmosphere ;
Scan not the source of all that makes earth
      comely ;
        Enough that light is here.

Question not love ; or pondering love's essence,
The wonder of his glory will confound
Those fair effects that issue from his presence ;
        But look around,
And thou wilt find the narrowest prospect
      spacious,
And dark perplexities serenely clear ;
Scan not the source of all that makes life
      gracious ;
        Enough that love is here.

NOVEMBER

Mourner, who wanderest gray and mute
O'er mouldering leaves and fallen fruit,
      Weep, unreproved !
Thou art not for thy sombre suit
      The less beloved.

Welcome as April's bridal tears,
Or the ripe smile September wears,
      Are thy grave eyes,
Made wistful with the agéd year's
      Dim memories.

Nineteenth Century.

Thine are the dawns of solemn sheen,
Through interwoven branches seen,
    As when doth smite
Through some cathedral's carven screen
    The altar's light.

Thou lendest darkness to the yew,
To distant hills a deeper blue ;
    Thy footsteps wake
Mosses to flower, when flowers are few
    In leafless brake.

Fair as her liveliest summer dress
The beech's silver nakedness,
    When red and gold,
That robed her for the storm's caress,
    Her feet enfold.

Through steel-blue clouds a gleaming wedge
Strikes on the berry-jewelled hedge
    And dusky wood,
On osiers smooth and tawny sedge
    And streams in flood.

And as a child's light laugh beguiles
Sorrow to lose herself in smiles,
    The redbreast's lay
Maketh the woodland's silent aisles
    Seem almost gay.

'Tis good to watch the loose clouds driven,
When the broad south their web hath riven,
    Or pace again
Beneath a calm snow-burdened heaven
    The darkening lane.

Strewn with the maple's moth-like seeds,
And catch the scent of smouldering weeds
　　　　O'er brown waves borne,
Of fresh-ploughed loam and silent meads
　　　　And cornfields shorn ;

'Tis good to feel thy tear drops fall
Upon the dead fern's quiet pall
　　　　Of purple mist,
When frost for their snow-burial
　　　　The wolds hath kissed ;

But best to watch—when deathlike eve
The pensive landscape doth bereave
　　　　Of short-lived day—
Thy great pathetic sunsets grieve
　　　　Their hearts away.

CONSERVATION

THOU, who from many a spray forlorn
Its ruddy jewelry hast torn,
　　　　Belovéd thrush !
From mountain-ash no need to fly,
At sight of me, to sanctuary
　　　　Of laurel-bush.

Plunder thy fill !—my garden yet
Is sweet with stock and mignonette,
　　　　With asters gay,
And of its plenty well can spare,
O prince of song, the frugal fare
　　　　It doth purvey.

Nineteenth Century.

Soon will the dahlia's pride lie dead,
The sunflower droop his kingly head,
   And pinched with cold
The lordly hollyhock repine
For still September's mild sunshine
   And moon of gold.

Then Winter with her wailful rains
Will weep o'er Autumn's gaunt remains,
   Or watch them lie
Stark in the snow's sepulchral dress,
Entombed within a featureless
   Gray vault of sky.

But when I sigh, dear mottled thief,
For crocus-flower and lilac-leaf
   Delaying long,
The vanished splendour of the tree
Will glow again, conserved by thee,
   In glorious song.

HAYESWATER

Enfolded in the mountain's naked arms,
 Where noonday wears a drearier look than
   night,
 And echo, like a shrinking anchorite,
 Wanders unseen, and shadowy strange alarms
Visit the soul ; there sunshine rarely warms
 The crags, but only random shafts of light
 Flit, while the black squalls shrilling from
   the height
 Shudder along the lake in scattering swarms.

Cradle of tempests, whence the whirlwind leaps
  To scourge the billows, till they writhe and
    rear
  Columns of hissing spray ; the wrinkled steeps
Scowl at the sullen moaning of the mere,
  And luminous against the dale-side drear,
  Ghostlike, the rainstorm's scanty vesture
    sweeps.

—>£-3<—

ILLUSION

When, in despite of care's dead weight,
And tarnished faith, and hope's decay,
A gladness stirs thee, delicate
As the first tremor of the Spring
Or thrill of love's awakening,
Ask it not whence—or it will shrink away.

So when the rainbow's transient smile
Cheereth heaven's gray and tearful face,
Look lightly on that tender wile ;
For if too hard in joy's excess,
Thou gaze, the specious loveliness
Will fade as doth a dream, and leave no trace.

—>£-3<—

TO THE REDBREAST

Minstrel of Autumn ! when a sadder sun
  Swoons night by night along the weeping
    west,
When thrush and merle, their wealth of love-
    song spent,
  Crouch shivering, each beside his ruined nest,

Nineteenth Century.

When, fluttering down, the dead leaves, one by
    one,
  Whisper o'er dying flowers a slow lament,
Then thou, bright bird, the latest and the best,
  Perched on the arm of some dismantled tree,
Dost utter from thy full and glowing breast
  Such rapturous strains of happy minstrelsy,
That neither mouldering leaves nor sobbing
    skies
  Can damp the faith in life that never dies.

Oliver Wendell Holmes

SUN AND SHADOW

As I look from the isle, o'er its billows of green
  To the billows of foam-crested blue,
Yon bark that afar in the distance is seen,
  Half dreaming, my eyes will pursue :
Now dark in the shadow, she scatters the spray
  As the chaff in the stroke of the flail ;
Now white as the sea-gull, she flies on her way,
  The sun gleaming bright on her sail.

Yet her pilot is thinking of dangers to shun,—
  Of breakers that whiten and roar ;
How little he cares, if in shadow or sun
  They see him that gaze from the shore !
He looks to the beacon that looms from the
    reef,
  To the rock that is under his lee,
As he drifts on the blast, like a wind-wafted leaf,
  O'er the gulfs of the desolate sea.

Thus drifting afar to the dim-vaulted caves
  Where life and its ventures are laid,
The dreamers who gaze while we battle the
    waves
  May see us in sunshine or shade ;

Yet true to our course, though our shadow
    grow dark,
We'll trim our broad sail as before,
And stand by the rudder that governs the bark,
    Nor ask how we look from the shore !

—⁖⁘⁖—

THE OLD MAN DREAMS

Oh, for one hour of youthful joy !
    Give back my twentieth spring !
I'd rather laugh a bright-haired boy,
    Than reign a gray-beard king !

Off with the wrinkled spoils of age,
    Away with learning's crown,
Tear out life's wisdom-written page,
    And dash its trophies down !

One moment let my life-blood stream
    From boyhood's fount of flame ;
Give me one giddy, reeling dream
    Of life all love and fame !

My listening angel heard the prayer,
    And, calmly smiling, said,
" If I but touch thy silvered hair,
    Thy hasty wish hath sped.

" But is there nothing in thy track
    To bid thee fondly stay,
While the swift seasons hurry back
    To find the wished-for day ? "

" Ah, truest soul of womankind,
   Without thee what were life?
One bliss I cannot leave behind,
   I'll take—my—precious—wife ! "

The angel took a sapphire pen,
   And wrote in rainbow dew,
" The man would be a boy again,
   And be a husband too ! "

" And is there nothing yet unsaid,
   Before the change appears?
Remember, all their gifts have fled
   With those dissolving years ! "

" Why, yes—for memory would recall
   My fond parental joys ;
I could not bear to leave them all—
   I'll take—my—girl—and—boys ! "

The smiling angel dropt his pen,—
   " Why, this will never do ;
The man would be a boy again,
   And be a father too ! "

And so I laughed—my laughter woke
   The household with its noise—
And wrote my dream, when morning broke,
   To please the grey-haired boys.

→>ɛ-3←—

Nineteenth Century.

"CALL HIM NOT OLD"

"CALL him not old, whose visionary brain
Holds o'er the past its undivided reign.
For him in vain the envious seasons roll
Who bears eternal summer in his soul.
If yet the minstrel's song, the poet's lay,
Spring with her birds, or children with their
    play,
Or maiden's smile, or heavenly dream of art,
Stir the warm life-drops creeping round his
    heart—
Turn to the record where his years are told—
Count his grey hairs—they cannot make him
    old !

Charles Kingsley

THE DELECTABLE DAY

The boy on the famous grey pony,
  Just bidding good-bye at the door,
Plucking up maiden heart for the fences
  Where his brother won honour of yore.

The walk to "the Meet" with fair children,
  And women as gentle as gay,—
Ah! how do we male hogs in armour
  Deserve such companions as they?

The afternoon's wander to windward,
  To meet the dear boy coming back;
And to catch, down the turns of the valley,
  The last weary chime of the pack.

The climb homeward by park and by moorland,
  And through the fir forests again,
While the south-west wind roars in the gloam-
    ing
  Like an ocean of seething champagne?

And at night the septette of Beethoven,
  And the grandmother by in her chair,
And the foot of all feet on the sofa
  Beating delicate time to the air.

Dainty Poems.

Ah, God! a poor soul can but thank Thee
  For such a delectable day!
Though the fury, the fool, and the swindler,
  To-morrow again have their way!

—⊹⊱⊰⊹—

MARGARET TO DOLCINO

Ask if I love thee? oh, smiles cannot tell
Plainer what tears are now showing too well.
Had I not loved thee, my sky had been clear:
Had I not loved thee, I had not been here,
            Weeping by thee.

Ask if I love thee? How else could I borrow
Pride from man's slander, and strength from
   my sorrow?
Laugh when they sneer at the fanatic's bride,
Knowing no bliss, save to toil and abide
            Weeping by thee.

—⊹⊱⊰⊹—

DOLCINO TO MARGARET

The world goes up and the world goes down,
  And the sunshine follows the rain;
And yesterday's sneer and yesterday's frown
  Can never come over again,
             Sweet wife;
No, never come over again.

Dainty Poems.

For woman is warm though man be cold,
  And the night will hallow the day;
Till the heart which at even was weary and old
  Can rise in the morning gay,
                   Sweet **wife**;
To its work in the morning gay.

A HOPE

TWIN stars, aloft in ether clear,
  Around each other roll alway,
Within one common atmosphere
  Of their own mutual light and day.

And myriad happy eyes are bent
  Upon their changeless love alway;
As strengthened by their one intent,
  They pour the flood of life and day.

So we through this world's waning night
  May, hand in hand, pursue our way;
Shed round us order, love, and light,
  And shine unto the perfect day.

H. W. Longfellow

THE BUILDING OF THE SHIP

"BUILD me straight, O worthy Master !
   Staunch and strong, a goodly vessel,
That shall laugh at all disaster,
   And with wave and whirlwind wrestle ! "

The merchant's word
Delighted the Master heard ;
For his heart was in his work, and the heart
Giveth grace unto every Art.
A quiet smile played round his lips,
As the eddies and dimples of the tide
Play round the bows of ships,
That steadily at anchor ride.
And with a voice that was full of glee,
He answered, " Ere long we will launch
A vessel as goodly, and strong, and staunch,
As ever weathered a wintry sea ! "

And first with nicest skill and art,
Perfect and finished in every part,
A little model the Master wrought,
Which should be to the larger plan
What the child is to the man,

Its counterpart in miniature ;
That with a hand more swift and sure
The greater labour might be brought
To answer to his inward thought.
And as he laboured, his mind ran o'er
The various ships that were built of yore,
And above them all, and strangest of all,
Towered the *Great Harry*, crank and tall,
Whose picture was hanging on the wall,
With bows and stern raised high in air,
And balconies hanging here and there,
And signal lanterns and flags afloat,
And eight round towers, like those that frown,
From some old castle, looking down
Upon the drawbridge and the moat.
And he said with a smile, " Our ship, I wis,
Shall be of another form than this ! "
It was of another form, indeed ;
Built for freight, and yet for speed,
A beautiful and gallant craft ;
Broad in the beam, that the stress of the blast,
Pressing down upon sail and mast,
Might not the sharp bows overwhelm ;
Broad in the beam, but sloping aft
With graceful curve and slow degrees,
That she might be docile to the helm,
And that the currents of parted seas,
Closing behind, with mighty force,
Might aid and not impede her course.

In the ship-yard stood the Master,
   With the model of the vessel,
That should laugh at all disaster,
   And with wave and whirlwind wrestle !

Nineteenth Century.

Covering many a rood of ground,
Lay the timber piled around ;
Timber of chestnut, and elm, and oak.
And scattered here and there, with these,
The knarred and crooked cedar knees ;
Brought from regions far away,
From Pascagoula's sunny bay,
And the banks of the roaring Roanoke !
Ah ! what a wondrous thing it is
To note how many wheels of toil
One thought, one word, can set in motion !
There's not a ship that sails the ocean,
But every climate, every soil,
Must bring its tribute, great or small,
And help to build the wooden wall !

The sun was rising o'er the sea,
And long the level shadows lay,
As if they, too, the beams would be
Of some great, airy argosy,
Framed and launched in a single day.
That silent architect, the sun,
Had hewn and laid them every one,
Ere the work of man was yet begun.
Beside the Master, when he spoke,
A youth, against an anchor leaning,
Listened to catch his slightest meaning.
Only the long waves, as they broke
In ripples on the pebbly beach,
Interrupted the old man's speech.

Beautiful they were, in sooth,
The old man and the fiery youth !
The old man, in whose busy brain

Many a ship that sailed the main
Was modelled o'er and o'er again ;—
The fiery youth, who was to be
The heir of his dexterity,
The heir of his house, and his daughter's hand,
When he had built and launched from land
What the elder head had planned.

"Thus," said he, "will we build this ship!
Lay square the blocks upon the slip,
And follow well this plan of mine.
Choose the timbers with greatest care ;
Of all that is unsound beware ;
For only what is sound and strong
To this vessel shall belong.
Cedar of Maine and Georgia pine
Here together shall combine.
A goodly frame, and a goodly fame,
And the UNION be her name !
For the day that gives her to the sea
Shall give my daughter unto thee !"

The Master's word
Enraptured the young man heard ;
And as he turned his face aside,
With a look of joy and a thrill of pride,
Standing before
Her father's door,
He saw the form of his promised bride.
The sun shone on her golden hair,
And her cheek was glowing fresh and fair,
With the breath of morn and the soft sea air
Like a beauteous barge was she,

Nineteenth Century.

Still at rest on the sandy beach,
Just beyond the billow's reach!
But he,
Was the restless, seething, stormy sea!

Ah, how skilful grows the hand
That obeyeth Love's command!
It is the heart, and not the brain,
That to the highest doth attain,
And he who followeth Love's behest
Far exceedeth all the rest!

Thus with the rising of the sun
Was the noble task begun,
And soon throughout the ship-yard's bounds
Were heard the intermingled sounds
Of axes and of mallets, plied
With vigorous arms on every side;
Plied so deftly and so well,
That ere the shadows of evening fell,
The keel of oak for a noble ship,
Scarfed and bolted, straight and strong,
Was lying ready, and stretched along
The blocks, well placed upon the slip.
Happy, thrice happy, every one
Who sees his labour well begun,
And not perplexed and multiplied,
By idly waiting for time and tide!

And when the hot, long day was o'er,
The young man at the Master's door
Sat with the maiden calm and still.
And within the porch, a little more

Removed beyond the evening chill,
The father sat, and told them tales
Of wrecks in the great September gales,
Of pirates upon the Spanish Main,
And ships that never came back again ;
The chance and change of a sailor's life,
Want and plenty, rest and strife,
His roving fancy, like the wind,
That nothing can stay and nothing can bind ;
And the magic charm of foreign lands,
With shadows of palms, and shining sands,
Where the tumbling surf,
O'er the coral reefs of Madagascar,
Washes the feet of the swarthy Lascar,
As he lies alone and asleep on the turf.
And the trembling maiden held her breath
At the tales of that awful, pitiless sea,
With all its terror and mystery,
The dim, dark sea, so like unto Death,
That divides and yet unites mankind !
And whenever the old man paused, a gleam
From the bowl of his pipe would awhile illume
The silent group in the twilight gloom,
And thoughtful faces, as in a dream ;
And for a moment one might mark
What had been hidden by the dark,
That the head of the maiden lay at rest,
Tenderly, on the young man's breast !

Day by day the vessel grew,
With timbers fashioned strong and true,
Stemson and keelson and sternson-knee,
Till, framed with perfect symmetry,

Nineteenth Century.

A skeleton ship rose up to view !
And around the bows and along the side
The heavy hammers and mallets plied,
Till after many a week, at length,
Wonderful for form and strength,
Sublime in its enormous bulk,
Loomed aloft the shadowy hulk !
And around it columns of smoke, upwreathing
Rose from the boiling, bubbling, seething
Caldron, that glowed,
And overflowed
With the black tar, heated for the sheathing.
And amid the clamours
Of clattering hammers,
He who listened heard now and then
The song of the Master and his men :—

" Build me straight, O worthy Master,
   Staunch and strong, a goodly vessel,
That shall laugh at all disaster,
   And with wave and whirlwind wrestle ! "

With oaken brace and copper band,
Lay the rudder on the sand,
That, like a thought, should have control
Over the movement of the whole ;
And near it the anchor, whose giant hand
Would reach down and grapple with the land,
And immovable and fast
Hold the great ship against the bellowing blast !
And at the bows an image stood,
By a cunning artist carved in wood,
With robes of white, that far behind
Seemed to be fluttering in the wind.

It was not shaped in a classic mould,
Not like a Nymph or Goddess of old,
Or Naiad rising from the water,
But modelled from the Master's daughter !
On many a dreary and misty night
'Twill be seen by the rays of the signal light,
Speeding along through the rain and the dark,
Like a ghost in its snow-white sark,
The pilot of some phantom bark,
Guiding the vessel, in its flight,
By a path none other knows aright.

Behold, at last,
Each tall and tapering mast
Is swung into its place ;
Shrouds and stays
Holding it firm and fast !

Long ago,
In the deer-haunted forests of Maine,
When upon mountain and plain
Lay the snow,
They fell,—those lordly pines !
Those grand, majestic pines !
'Mid shouts and cheers
The jaded steers,
Panting beneath the goad,
Dragged down the weary, winding road
Those captive kings so straight and tall,
To be shorn of their streaming hair,
And, naked and bare,
To feel the stress and the strain
Of the wind and the reeling main,
Whose roar

Nineteenth Century.

Would remind them for evermore
Of their native forests they should not see again.
And everywhere
The slender, graceful spars
Poise aloft in the air,
And at the mast head,
White, blue, and red,
A flag unrolls the stripes and stars.
Ah! when the wanderer lonely, friendless,
In foreign harbours shall behold
That flag unrolled,
'Twill be as a friendly hand
Stretched out from his native land,
Filling his heart with memories sweet and end-
    less.

All is finished! and at length
Has come the bridal day
Of beauty and of strength.
To-day the vessel shall be launched!
With fleecy clouds the sky is blanched,
And o'er the bay,
Slowly, in all his splendours dight,
The great sun rises to behold the sight.
The ocean old,
Centuries old,
Strong as youth, and as uncontrolled,
Paces restless to and fro,
Up and down the sands of gold.
His beating heart is not at rest;
And far and wide,
With ceaseless flow,
His beard of snow
Heaves with the heaving of his breast.

He waits impatient for his bride.
There she stands,
With her foot upon the sands,
Decked with flags and streamers gay,
In honour of her marriage day,
Her snow-white signals fluttering, blending,
Round her like a veil descending,
Ready to be
The bride of the grey, old sea.

On the deck another bride
Is standing by her lover's side.
Shadows from the flags and shrouds,
Like the shadows cast by clouds,
Broken by many a sudden fleck,
Fall around them on the deck.

The prayer is said,
The service read,
The joyous bridegroom bows his head,
And in tears the good old Master,
Shakes the brown hand of his son,
Kisses his daughter's glowing cheek
In silence, for he cannot speak,
And ever faster
Down his own the tears begin to run.
The worthy pastor—
The shepherd of that wandering flock
That has the ocean for its wold,
That has the vessel for its fold,
Leaping ever from rock to rock—
Spake, with accents mild and clear,
Words of warning, words of cheer,
But tedious to the bridegroom's ear.
He knew the chart

Nineteenth Century.

Of the sailor's heart,
All its pleasures and its griefs,
All its shallows and rocky reefs,
All those secret currents, that flow
With such resistless undertow,
And lift and drift, with terrible force,
The will from its moorings and its course.
Therefore he spake, and thus said he :—

'' Like unto ships far off at sea,
Outward or homeward bound, are we.
Before, behind, and all around,
Floats and swings the horizon's bound,
Seems at its distant rim to rise
And climb the crystal wall of the skies,
And then again to turn and sink,
As if we could slide from its outer brink.
Ah ! it is not the sea,
It is not the sea that sinks and shelves,
But ourselves
That rock and rise
With endless and uneasy motion,
Now touching the very skies,
Now sinking into the depths of ocean.
Ah ! if our souls but poise and swing
Like the compass in its brazen ring,
Ever level, and ever true
To the toil and the task we have to do,
We shall sail securely, and safely reach
The Fortunate Isles, on whose shining beach
The sights we see, and the sounds we hear,
Will be those of joy and not of fear ! "

Then the Master,
With a gesture of command,

Waved his hand;
And at the word,
Loud and sudden there was heard,
All around them and below,
The sound of hammers, blow on blow,
Knocking away the shores and spurs.
And see ! she stirs !
She starts,—she moves,—she seems to feel
The thrill of life along her keel,
And, spurning with her foot the ground,
With one exulting, joyous bound,
She leaps into the ocean's arms !
And lo ! from the assembled crowd
There rose a shout prolonged and loud,
That to the ocean seemed to say,—
"Take her, O bridegroom, old and grey,
Take her to thy protecting arms,
With all her youth and all her charms !"

How beautiful she is ! How fair
She lies within those arms that press
Her form with many a soft caress
Of tenderness and watchful care !
Sail forth into the sea, O ship !
Through wind and wave, right onward steer !
The moistened eye, the trembling lip,
Are not the signs of doubt or fear.

Sail forth into the sea of life,
O gentle, loving, trusting wife,
And safe from all adversity
Upon the bosom of that sea
Thy comings and thy goings be !
For gentleness and love and trust
Prevail o'er angry wave and gust ;

Nineteenth Century.

And in the wreck of noble lives
Something immortal still survives!

Thou, too, sail on, O Ship of State!
Sail on, O UNION, strong and great!
Humanity, with all its fears,
With all the hopes of future years,
Is hanging breathless on thy fate!
We know what Master laid thy keel,
What Workmen wrought thy ribs of steel,
Who made each mast, and sail, and rope,
What anvils rang, what hammers beat,
In what a forge and what a heat
Were shaped the anchors of thy hope!
Fear not each sudden sound and shock,
'Tis of the wave and not the rock;
'Tis but the flapping of the sail,
And not a rent made by the gale!
In spite of rock and tempest's roar,
In spite of false lights on the shore,
Sail on, nor fear to breast the sea!
Our hearts, our hopes, are all with thee,
Our faith triumphant o'er our fears,
Are all with thee,—are all with thee!

WEARINESS

O LITTLE feet! that such long years
Must wander on through hopes and fears,
  Must ache and bleed beneath your load;
I, nearer to the Wayside Inn
Where toil shall cease and rest begin,
  Am weary, thinking of your road!

O little hands! that, weak or strong,
Have still to serve or rule so long,
　Have still so long to give or ask;
I, who so much with book and pen
Have toiled among my fellow-men,
　Am weary, thinking of your task.

O little hearts! that throb and beat
With such impatient, feverish heat,
　Such limitless and strong desires;
Mine that so long has glowed and burned,
With passions into ashes turned
　Now covers and conceals its fires.

O little souls! as pure and white
And crystalline as rays of light
　Direct from heaven, their source divine;
Refracted through the mist of years,
How red my setting sun appears,
　How lurid looks this soul of mine!

THE CHILDREN'S HOUR

BETWEEN the dark and the daylight,
　When the night is beginning to lower,
Comes a pause in the day's occupations
　That is known as the Children's Hour.

I hear in the chamber above me
　The patter of little feet,
The sound of a door that is opened,
　And voices soft and sweet.

Nineteenth Century.

From my study I see in the lamplight,
  Descending the broad hall stair,
Grave Alice and laughing Allegra,
  And Edith with golden hair.

A whisper and then a silence;
  Yet I know by their merry eyes
They are plotting and planning together
  To take me by surprise.

A sudden rush from the stairway,
  A sudden raid from the hall!
By three doors left unguarded
  They enter my castle wall!

They climb up into my turret
  O'er the arms and back of my chair;
If I try to escape they surround me;
  They seem to be everywhere.

They almost devour me with kisses,
  Their arms about me entwine,
Till I think of the Bishop of Bingen
  In his Mouse Tower on the Rhine!

Do you think, O blue-eyed Banditti,
  Because you have scaled the wall,
Such an old moustache as I am
  Is not a match for you all!

I have you fast in my fortress,
  And will not let you depart,
But put you down into the dungeon
  In the round-tower of my heart.

And there will I keep you for ever,
   Yes, for ever and a day,
Till the walls shall crumble to ruin,
   And moulder in dust away !

→&·&←

CHILDREN

Come to me, O ye children !
   For I hear you at your play,
And the questions that perplexed me
   Have vanished quite away.

Ye open the eastern windows,
   That look towards the sun,
Where thoughts are singing swallows,
   And the brooks of morning run.

In your hearts are the birds and the sunshine,
   In your thoughts the brooklet's flow,
But in mine is the wind of Autumn,
   And the first fall of the snow.

Ah ! what would the world be to us,
   If the children were no more?
We should dread the desert behind us
   Worse than the dark before.

What the leaves are to the forest,
   With light and air for food,
Ere their sweet and tender juices
   Have been hardened into wood,—

Nineteenth Century.

That to the world are children ;
  Through them it feels the glow
Of a brighter and sunnier climate
  Than reaches the trunks below.

Come to me, O ye children !
  And whisper in my ear
What the birds and the winds are singing
  In your sunny atmosphere.

For what are all our contrivings,
  And the wisdom of our books,
When compared with your caresses,
  And the gladness of your looks ?

Ye are better than all the ballads
  That ever were sung or said ;
For ye are living poems,
  And all the rest are dead.

James Russell Lowell

———

MY LOVE

I.

NOT as all other women are
Is she that to my soul is dear ;
Her glorious fancies come from far,
Beneath the silver evening star,
And yet her heart is ever near.

II.

Great feelings hath she of her own,
Which lesser souls may never know ;
God giveth them to her alone,
And sweet they are as any tone
Wherewith the wind may choose to blow.

III.

Yet in herself she dwelleth not,
Although no home were half so fair ;
No simplest duty is forgot,
Life hath no dim and lowly spot
That doth not in her sunshine share.

Dainty Poems.

IV.

She doeth little kindnesses,
Which most leave undone, or despise:
For naught that sets one heart at ease,
And giveth happiness or peace,
Is low-esteemèd in her eyes.

V.

She hath no scorn of common things,
And, though she seem of other birth,
Round us her heart entwines and clings,
And patiently she folds her wings
To tread the humble paths of earth.

VI.

Blessing she is : God made her so,
And deeds of week-day holiness
Fall from her noiseless as the snow,
Nor hath she ever chanced to know
That aught were easier than to bless.

VII.

She is most fair, and thereunto
Her life doth rightly harmonise ;
Feeling or thought that was not true
Ne'er made less beautiful the blue
Unclouded heaven of her eyes.

VIII.

She is a woman : one in whom
The spring-time of her childish years
Hath never lost its fresh perfume,
Though knowing well that life hath room
For many blights and many tears.

IX.

I love her with a love as still
As a broad river's peaceful might,
Which, by high tower and lowly mill,
Goes wandering at its own will,
And yet doth ever flow aright.

X.

And on its full, deep breast serene,
Like quiet isles my duties lie ;
It flows around them and between,
And makes them fresh and fair and green,
Sweet homes wherein to live and die.

→⥿⥿←

SHE CAME AND WENT

As a twig trembles, which a bird
  Lights on to sing, then leaves unbent,
So is my memory thrilled and stirred ;—
  I only know she came and went.

As clasps some lake, by gusts unriven
  The blue dome's measureless content,
So my soul held that moment's heaven ;—
  I only know she came and went.

As, at one bound, our swift spring heaps
  The orchards full of bloom and scent,
So clove her May my wintry sleeps ;—
  I only know she came and went.

Nineteenth Century.

An angel stood and met my gaze,
 Through the low doorway of my tent;
The tent is struck, the vision stays;—
 I only know she came and went.

Oh, when the room grows slowly dim,
 And life's last oil is nearly spent,
One gush of light these eyes will brim,
 Only to think she came and went.

LONGING

Of all the myriad moods of mind
 That through the soul come thronging,
Which one was e'er so dear, so kind,
 So beautiful as Longing?
The thing we long for, that we are
 For one transcendent moment,
Before the Present, poor and bare,
 Can make its sneering comment.

Still, through our paltry stir and strife,
 Glows down the wished Ideal,
And Longing moulds in clay what Life
 Carves in the marble Real;
To let the new life in, we know,
 Desire must ope the portal;—
Perhaps the longing to be so
 Helps make the soul immortal.

Longing is God's fresh heavenward will
 With our poor earthward striving;
We quench it that we may be still
 Content with merely living;

But would we learn that heart's full scope
　Which we are hourly wronging,
Our lives must climb from hope to hope
　And realise our longing.

Ah ! let us hope that to our praise
　Good God not only reckons
The moments when we tread His ways,
　But when the spirit beckons,—
That some slight good is also wrought
　Beyond self-satisfaction,
When we are simply good in thought,
　Howe'er we fail in action.

SONG

O MOONLIGHT deep and tender,
　A year and more agone,
Your mist of golden splendour
　Round my betrothal shone !

O elm-leaves dark and dewy,
　The very same ye seem,
The low wind trembles through ye,
　Ye murmur in my dream !

O river, dim with distance,
　Flow thus for ever by,
A part of my existence
　Within your heart doth lie !

Nineteenth Century.

O stars, ye saw our meeting,
  Two beings and one soul,
Two hearts so madly beating
  To mingle and be whole !

O happy night, deliver
  Her kisses back to me,
Or keep them all, and give her
  A blissful dream of me !

George MacDonald

WHERE did you come from, baby dear?
Out of the everywhere into here.

Where did you get those eyes of blue?
Out of the sky as I came through.

What makes the light in them sparkle and spin
Some of the starry twinkles left in.

Where did you get that little tear?
I found it waiting when I got here.

What makes your forehead so smooth and high?
A soft hand stroked it as I went by.

What makes your cheek like a warm white rose?
I saw something better than anyone knows.

Whence that three-cornered smile of bliss?
Three angels gave me at once a kiss.

Where did you get this pearly ear?
God spoke, and it came out to hear.

Where did you get those arms and hands?
Love made itself into bonds and bands.

Feet, whence did you come, you darling things?
From the same box as the cherubs' wings.

How did they all just come to be you?
God thought about me, and so I grew.

But how did you come to us, you dear?
God thought about you, and so I am here.

—>§·§<—

TWO IN ONE

I.

Were thou and I the white pinions
  On some eager, heaven-born dove,
Swift would we mount to the old dominions,
  To our rest of old, my love!

Were thou and I trembling strands
  In music's enchanted line,
We would wait and wait for magic hands
  To untwist the magic twine.

Were we two sky-tints, thou and I,
  Thou the golden, I the red;
We would quiver and glow and darken and die,
  And love until we were dead!

Nearer than wings of one dove,
  Than tones or colours in chord,
We are one—and safe, and for ever, my love,
  Two thoughts in the heart of one Lord.

PICTURE SONGS

A PALE green sky is gleaming ;
  The steely stars are few ;
The moorland pond is steaming
  A mist of gray and blue.

Along the pathway lonely
  My horse is walking slow ;
Three living creatures only,
  He, I, and a home-bound crow !

The moon is hardly shaping
  Her circle in the fog ;
A dumb stream is escaping
  Its prison in the bog.

But in my heart are ringing
  Tones of a lofty song ;
A voice that I know, is singing,
  And my heart all night must long.

II.

Over a shining land—
  Once such a land I knew—
Over its sea, by a soft wind fanned,
  The sky is all white and blue.

The waves are kissing the shores,
  Murmuring love and for ever ;
A boat gleams green, and its timeful oars
  Flash out of the level river.

Oh to be there with thee
  And the sun on wet sands, my love !

Nineteenth Century.

With the shining river, the sparkling sea,
　And the radiant sky above!

III.

The autumn winds are sighing
　Over land and sea ;
The autumn woods are dying
　Over hill and lea ;
And my heart is sighing, dying,
　Maiden, for thee.

The autumn clouds are flying
　Homeless over me ;
The nestless birds are crying
　In the naked tree ;
And my heart is flying, crying,
　Maiden, to thee.

The autumn sea is crawling
　Up the chilly shore ;
The thin-voiced firs are calling
　Ghostily evermore :
Maiden, maiden ! I am falling
　Dead at thy door.

IV.

The waters are rising and flowing
　Over the weedy stone—
Over it, over it going :
　It is never gone.

Waves upon waves of weeping
　Went over the ancient pain ;
Glad waves go over it leaping—
　Still it rises again !

Eric Mackay

LOVE LETTERS OF A VIOLINIST

LETTER VIII.—A VISION

I.

Yes, I will tell thee what, a week ago,
I dreamt of thee, and all the joy therein
Which I conceiv'd, and all the holy din
Of throbbing music, which appear'd to flow
From room to room, as if to make me know
The power thereof to lead me out of sin.

II.

Methought I saw thee in a ray of light,
This side a grove—a dream within a dream—
With eyes of tender pleading, and the gleam
Of far-off summers in thy tresses bright ;
And I did tremble at the gracious sight,
As one who sees a naiad in a stream.

III.

I followed thee. I knew that, in the wood,
Where thus we met, there was a trysting place.
I follow'd thee, as mortals in a chase
Follow the deer. I knew that it was good
To track thy step, and promptly understood
The fitful blush that flutter'd to thy face.

156

Dainty Poems.

IV.

I followed thee to where a brook did run
  Close to a grot ; and there I knelt to thee.
  And then a score of birds flew over me,—
Birds which arrived because the day was done,
To sing the Sanctus of the setting sun ;
  And then I heard thy voice upon the lea.

V.

" Follow ! " it cried.   I rose and follow'd fast ;
  And, in my dream, I felt the dream was true,
  And that, full soon, Titania, with her crew
Of imps and fays, would meet me on the blast.
But this was hindered ; and I quickly passed
  Into the valley where the cedars grew.

VI.

And what a scene, O God ! and what repose,
  And what sad splendour in the burning west .
  A languid sun low-dropping to his rest,
And incense rising, as of old it rose,
To do him honour at the daylight's close,—
  The birds entranced, and all the winds
    repress'd.

VII.

I followed thee.   I came to where a shrine
  Stood in the trees, and where an oaken gate
  Swung in the air, so turbulent of late.
I touch'd thy hand ; it quiver'd into mine ;
And then I look'd into thy face benign,
  And saw the smile for which the angels wait.

VIII.

And lo ! the moon had sailed into the main
  Of that blue sky, as if therein did poise
  A silver boat ; and then a tuneful noise
Broke from the copse where late a breeze was
    slain ;
And nightingales, in ecstasy of pain,
  Did break their hearts with singing the old
    joys.

IX.

"Is this the spot?" I cried, "is this the spot
  Where I must tell thee all my heart's desire?
  Is this the time when I must drink the fire,
And eat the snow, and find it fever-hot?
I freeze with heat, and yet I fear it not ;
  And all my pulses thrill me like a lyre."

X.

A wondrous light was thrown upon thy face ;
  It was the light within ; it was the ray
  Of thine own soul. And then a voice did say,
"Glory to God the King, and Jesu's grace
Here and hereafter ! " And about the place
  A radiance shone surpassing that of day.

XI.

It was thy voice. It was the voice I prize
  More than the sound of April in the dales,
  More than the songs of larks and nightingales,
And more than teachings of the worldly-wise.
"Glory to God," it said, " for, in the skies,
  And here on earth, 'tis He alone prevails."

Nineteenth Century.

XII.

And then I asked thee: "Shall I tell thee now
  All that I think of when, by land and sea,
  The days and nights illume the world for me?
And how I muse on marriage, as I bow,
In God's own places, with a throbbing brow?
  And how, at night, I dream of kissing thee?"

XIII.

But thou did'st answer: "First behold this man!
  He is thy lord, for love's and lady's sake;
  He is thy master or I much mistake."
And I perceiv'd, hard by, a phantom wan
And wild and kingly, who did, walking, span
  The open space that lay beside the brake.

XIV.

It was Beethoven. It was he who came
  From monstrous shades, to journey yet awhile
  In pleasant nooks, and vainly seek the smile
Of one lov'd woman—she to whom his fame
Had been a glory had she sought the same,
  And lov'd a soul so grand, so free from guile.

XV.

It was the Kaiser of the land of song,
  The giant-singer who did storm the gates
  Of Heaven and Hell, a man to whom the Fates
Were fierce as furies, and who suffer'd wrong
And ached and bore it, and was brave and
    strong,
  But gaunt as Ocean when its rage abates.

XVI.

I knew his tread.   I knew him by his look
  Of pent-up sorrow—by his hair unkempt
And torn attire—and by his smile exempt
  From all but pleading.   Yet his body shook
With some great joy; and onward he betook
  His echoing steps the way that I had dreamt.

XVII.

I bow'd my head.   The lordly being pass'd.
  He was my king, and I did bow to him.
  And when I rais'd mine eyes they were as dim
As tears could make them.   And the moon,
    aghast,
Glared in the sky; and westward came a blast
  Which shook the earth like shouts of cherubim.

XVIII.

I held my breath.   I could have fled the place,
  As men have fled before the wrath of God.
  But I beheld my Lady where she trod
The darken'd path; and I did cry apace:
"Help me, my Lady!" and thy lustrous face
  Gladden'd the air, and quicken'd all the sod.

XIX.

Then did I hear again that voice of cheer.
  "Lovest thou me," it said, "or music best?"
  I seized thy hand, I drew thee to my breast.
"Thee, only thee!" I cried.   "From year to
    year,
Thee, only thee—not fame!"   And silver-clear,
  Thy voice responded: "God will grant the
    rest."

XX.

I kissed thine eyes. I kissed them where the
blue
  Peep'd smiling forth ; and proudly as before
  I heard the tones that thrill'd me to the core.
"If thou love me," they said, "if thou be true,
Thou shalt have fame and love, and music too!"
  Entranced I kiss'd the lips that I adore.

—⧉—

LETTER IX.—TO-MORROW

O Love ! O Love ! O Gateway of Delight !
  Thou porch of peace, thou pageant of the
    prime
  Of all God's creatures ! I am here to climb
Thine upward steps, and daily and by night
To gaze beyond them, and to search aright
  The far-off splendour of thy track sublime.

II.

For, in thy precincts, on the further side,
  Beyond the turret where the bells are rung,
  Beyond the chapel where the rites are sung,
There is a garden fit for any bride.
O Love ! by thee, by thee are sanctified
  The joys thereof to keep our spirits young.

III.

By thee, dear Love ! by thee, if all be well—
  And we be wise enough to own the touch
  Of some bright folly that has thrill'd us
    much—
By thee, till death, we may regain the spell
Of wizard Merlin, and in every dell
  Confront a Muse, and bow to it as such.

IV.

Love! Happy Love! Behold me where I stand
  This side thy portal, with my straining eyes
  Turn'd to the Future. Cloudless are the skies,
And, far a down the road which thou hast spann'd,
I see the groves of that elected land
  Which is the place I call my paradise.

V.

But what is this? The plains are known to me,
  The hills are known, the fields, the little fence,
  The noisy brook as clear as innocence,
And this old oak, the wonder of the lea,
Which stops the wind to know if there shall be
  Sorrow for men, or pride, or recompense.

VI.

I know these things, yet hold it little blame
  To know them not, though in their proud array,
  The flowers advance to make the world so gay.
Ah, what a change! The things I know by name
Look unfamiliar all, and, like a flame,
  The roses burn upon the hedge to-day.

VII.

The grass is velvet. There are pearls thereon,
  And golden signs, and braid that doth appear
  Made for a bridal. This is fairy gear
If I mistake not. I shall know anon.
Nature herself will teach me how to con
  The new-found words to thank the glowing
    year.

VIII.

This is the path that led me to the brook;
  And this the mead, and this the mossy slope,
  And this the place where breezes did elope

With giddy moths, enamour'd of a look ;
And here I sat alone, or with a book,
  Dreaming the dreams of constancy and hope.

IX.

I loved the river well ; but not till now
  Did I perceive the marvels of the shore.
  This is a cave, and this an emerald floor ;
And here Sir Eglantine might make a vow,
And here a king, a guilty king, might bow
  Before a child, and break his word no more.

X.

The day is dying. I shall see him die,
  And I shall watch the sunset and the red
  Of all that splendour when the day is dead.
And I shall see the stars upon the sky,
And think them torches that are lit on high
  To light the lord Apollo to his bed.

XI.

And sweet To-morrow, like a golden bark,
  Will call for me, and lead me on apace
  To where I shall behold, in all her grace,
Mine own true Lady, whom a happy lark
Did late salute, appointing, after dark,
  A nightingale to carol in his place.

XII.

Oh, come to me ! oh, come, belovèd day,
  O sweet To-morrow ! Youngest of the sons
  Of old King Time, to whom Creation runs
As men to God. Oh, quickly with thy ray
Anoint my head, and teach me how to pray,
  As gentle Jesus taught the little ones.

XIII.

I am aweary of the waiting hours,
  I am aweary of the tardy night.
  The hungry moments rob me of delight,
The crawling minutes steal away my powers ;
And I am sick at heart, as one who cowers,
  In lonely haunts, remov'd from human sight.

XIV.

How shall I think the night was meant for
    sleep,
  When I must count the dreadful hours
    thereof,
  And cannot beat them down, or bid them doff
Their hateful masks? A man may wake and
    weep
From hour to hour, and, in the silence deep,
  See shadows move, and almost hear them
    scoff.

XV.

Oh, come to me, To-morrow ! like a friend,
  And not as one who bideth for the clock.
  Be swift to come, and I will hear thee knock,
And though the night refuse to make an end
Of her dull peace, I promptly will descend
  And let thee in, and thank thee for the shock.

XVI.

Dear, good To-morrow ! in my life, till now,
  I did not think to need thee quite so soon.
  I did not think that I should hate the moon,
Or new or old, or that my fevered brow
Requir'd the sun to cool it. I will bow
  To this new day, that he may grant the boon.

Nineteenth Century.

XVII.

Yes, 'twill consent. The day will dawn at last.
    Day and the tide approach. They cannot rest.
    They must approach. They must by every test
Of all men's knowledge, neither slow nor fast,
Approach and front us. When the night is past,
    The morrow's dawn will lead me to my quest.

XVIII.

Then shall I tremble greatly and be glad,
    For I shall meet my true-love all alone,
    And none shall tell me of her dainty zone,
And none shall say how sweetly she is clad ;
But I shall know it. Men may call me mad ;
    But I shall know how bright the world has
      grown.

XIX.

There is a grammar of the lips and eyes,
    And I have learnt it. There are tokens sure
    Of trust in love ; and I have found them pure.
Is love the guerdon then? Is love the prize?
It is ! It is ! We find it in the skies,
    And here on earth 'tis all that will endure.

XX.

All things for love. All things in some divine
    And wish'd for way, conspire as Nature
      knows,
    To some great good. Where'er a daisy grows
There grows a joy. The forest-trees combine
To talk of peace when mortals would repine ;
    And he is false to God who flouts the rose.

LETTER XII.—VICTORY

I.

Now have I reach'd the goal of my desire,
For thou hast sworn—as sweetly as a bell
Makes out its chime—the oath I love to tell,
The fealty-oath of which I never tire.
The lordly forest seems a giant's lyre,
And sings, and rings, the thoughts that o'er
it swell.

II.

The air is fill'd with voices. I have found
Comfort at last, enthralment, and a joy
Past all belief; a peace without alloy.
There is a splendour all about the ground
As if from Eden, when the world was drown'd,
Something had come which death could not
destroy.

III.

It seems, indeed, as if to me were sent
A smile from Heaven—as if to-day the clods
Were lined with silk—the trees divining rods,
And roses gems for some high tournament.
I should not be so proud, or so content,
If I could sup, to-night, with all the gods.

IV.

A shrinèd saint would change his place with me
If he but knew the worth of what I feel.
He is enrobed indeed, and for his weal
Hath much concern ; but how forlorn is he !
How pale his pomp ! He cannot sue to thee,
But I am sainted every time I kneel.

Nineteenth Century.

v.

I walk'd abroad, to-day, ere yet the dark
　　Had left the hills, and down the beaten road
　　I saunter'd forth a mile from mine abode.
I heard, afar, the watchdog's sudden bark,
And, near at hand, the tuning of a lark,
　　Safe in its nest, but weighted with an ode.

vi.

The moon was pacing up the sky serene,
　　Pallid and pure, as if she late had shown
　　Her outmost side, and fear'd to make it
　　　known;
And, like a nun, she gazed upon the scene
From bars of cloud that seemed to stand be-
　　tween,
　　And pray'd and smiled, and smiled and
　　　pray'd alone.

vii.

The stars had fled.　Not one remain'd behind
　　To warn or comfort; or to make amends
　　For hope delay'd,—for ecstasy that ends
At dawn's approach.　The firmament was blind
Of all its eyes; and, wanton up the wind,
　　There came the shuddering that the twilight
　　　sends.

viii.

The hills exulted at the Morning's birth,—
　　And clouds assembled, quick, as heralds run
　　Before a king to say the fight is won.
The rich, warm daylight fell upon the earth
Like wine outpour'd in madness, or in mirth,
　　To celebrate the rising of the sun.

IX.

And when the soaring lark had done his prayer,
  The holy thing, self-poised amid the blue
  Of that great sky, did seem, a space or two,
To pause and think, and then did clip the air
And dropped to earth to claim his guerdon there.
  "Thank God!" I cried, "My dearest dream
    is true!"

X.

I was too happy, then, to leap and dance;
  But I could ponder; I could gaze and gaze
  From earth to sky and back to woodland ways.
The bird had thrill'd my heart, and cheer'd my
    glance,
For he had found to-day his nest-romance,
  And lov'd a mate, and crown'd her with his
    praise.

XI.

O Love! my Love! I would not for a throne,
  I would not for the thrones of all the kings
  Who yet have liv'd, or for a seraph's wings,
Or for the nod of Jove when night hath flown,
Consent to rule an empire all alone.
  No! I must have the grace of our two rings.

XII.

I must possess thee from the crowning curl
  Down to the feet, and from the beaming eye
  Down to the bosom where my treasures lie.
From blush to blush, and from the rows of
    pearl
That light thy smile, I must possess thee, girl,
  And be thy lord and master till I die.

Nineteenth Century.

XIII.

This, and no less: the keeper of thy fame,
  The proud controller of each silken tress,
  And each dear item of thy loveliness,
And every oath, and every dainty name
Known to a bride: a picture in a frame
  Of golden hair, to turn to and caress.

XIV.

And though I know thee prone, in vacant hours,
  To laugh and talk with those who circumvent
  And make mad speeches; though I know
      the bent
Of some such men, and though in ladies' bowers
They brag of swords—I know my proven powers;
  I know myself and thee, and am content.

XV.

I know myself; and why should I demur?
  The lily, bowing to the breeze's play,
  Is not forgetful of the sun in May.
She is his nymph, and with a servitor
She doth but jest. The sun looks down at her,
  And knows her true, and loves her day by day.

XVI.

E'en so I thee, O Lady of my Heart!
  O Lady white as lilies on the lea,
  And fair as foam upon the ocean free
Whereon the sun hath sent a shining dart!
E'en so I love thee, blameless as thou art,
  And with my soul's desire I compass thee.

XVII.

For thou art Woman in the sweetest sense
  Of true endowment, and a bride indeed
  Fit for Apollo.   This is Woman's need :
To be a beacon when the air is dense,
A bower of peace, a life-long recompense—
  This is the sum of Woman's worldly creed.

XVIII.

And what is Man the while ? And what his will ?
  And what the furtherance of his earthly hope ?
  To turn to Faith, to turn, as to a rope
A drowning sailor ; all his blood to spill
For One he loves, to keep her out of ill—
  This is the will of Man, and this his scope.

XIX.

'Tis like the tranquil sea, that knows anon
  It can be wild, and keep away from home
  A thousand ships—and lash itself to foam—
And beat the shore, and all that lies thereon—
And catch the thunder ere the flash has gone
  Forth from the cloud that spans it like a
    dome.

XX.

This is the will of Man, and this is mine.
  But lo ! I love thee more than wealth or fame,
  More than myself, and more than those who
    came
With Christ's commission from the goal divine.
Soul of my soul, and mine as I am thine,
  I cling to thee, my Life ! as fire to flame.

Nineteenth Century.

PHILOMEL

Lo, as a minstrel at the court of Love,
　The nightingale, who knows his mate is nigh,
Thrills into rapture; and the stars above
　Look down, affrighted, as they would reply.
　There is contagion, and I know not why,
In all this clamour, all this fierce delight,
　As if the sunset, when the day did swoon,
　Had drawn some wild confession from the
　　moon.
Have wrongs been done? Have crimes enacted
　been
To shame the weird retirement of the night?
　O clamorous bird! O sad, sweet nightingale!
Withhold thy voice, and blame not Beauty's
　queen—
　She may be pure, though dumb: and she is
　　pale,
And wears a radiance on her brow serene.

THE WAKING OF THE LARK
I.

O bonnie bird, that in the brake, exultant
　　dost prepare thee—
As poets do whose thoughts are true, for wings
　　that will upbear thee—
　　Oh! tell me, tell me, bonnie bird,
　　Canst thou not pipe of hope deferred?
Or canst thou sing of naught but Spring among
　　the golden meadows?

171

II.

Methinks a bard (and thou art one) should suit
    his song to sorrow,
And tell of pain, as well as gain, that waits us on
    the morrow ;
    But thou art not a prophet, thou,
    If naught but joy can touch thee now ;
If, in thy heart, thou hast no vow that speaks of
    Nature's anguish.

III.

Oh ! I have held my sorrows dear, and felt, tho'
    poor and slighted,
The songs we love are those we hear when love
    is unrequited.
    But thou art still the slave of dawn,
    And canst not sing till night be gone,
Till o'er the pathway of the fawn the sunbeams
    shine and quiver.

IV.

Thou art the minion of the sun that rises in his
    splendour,
And canst not spare for Dian fair the songs that
    should attend her.
    The moon, so sad and silver-pale,
    Is mistress of the nightingale ;
And thou wilt sing on hill and dale no ditties in
    the darkness.

V.

For Queen and King thou wilt not spare one
    note of thine outpouring ;
Thou art as free as breezes be on Nature's velvet
    flooring.

Nineteenth Century.

The daisy, with its hood undone,
The grass, the sunlight, and the sun—
These are the joys, thou holy one, that pay thee
    for thy singing.

VI.

Oh, hush! Oh, hush! how wild a gush of
    rapture in the distance,—
A roll of rhymes, a toll of chimes, a cry for love's
    assistance;
    A sound that wells from happy throats,
    A flood of song where beauty floats,
And where our thoughts, like golden boats, do
    seem to cross a river.

VII.

This is the advent of the lark—the priest in gray
    apparel—
Who doth prepare to trill in air his sinless
    summer carol;
    This is the prelude to the lay
    The birds did sing in Cæsar's day,
And will again, for aye and aye, in praise of
    God's creation.

VIII.

O dainty thing, on wonder's wing, by life and
    love elated,
Oh! sing aloud from cloud to cloud, till day
    be consecrated;
    Till from the gateways of the morn,
    The sun, with all his light unshorn,
His robes of darkness round him torn, doth
    scale the lofty heavens!

MIRAGE

I.

'Tis a legend of a lover,
'Tis a ballad to be sung,
In the gloaming,—under cover,—
By a minstrel who is young;
By a singer who has passion, and who sways
us with his tongue.

II.

I, who know it, think upon it,
Not unhappy, tho' in tears,
And I gather in a sonnet
All the glory of the years;
And I kiss and clasp a shadow when the
substance disappears.

III.

Ah! I see her as she faced me,
In the sinless summer days,
When her little hands embraced me,
And I saddened at her gaze,
Thinking, Sweet One! will she love me when
we walk in other ways?

IV.

Will she cling to me as kindly
When the childish faith is lost?
Will she pray for me as blindly,
Or but weigh the wish and cost,
Looking back on our lost Eden from the girl-
hood she has cross'd?

Nineteenth Century.

V.

Oh! I swear by all I honour,
 By the graves that I endow,
By the grace I set upon her,
 That I meant the early vow,—
Meant it much as men and women mean the
 same thing spoken now.

VI.

But her maiden troth is broken,
 And her mind is ill at ease,
And she sends me back no token
 From her home beyond the seas;
And I know, though nought is spoken, that
 she thanks me on her knees.

VII.

Yes, for pardon freely granted;
 For she wrong'd me, understand.
And my life is disenchanted,
 As I wander through the land
With the sorrows of dark morrows that await
 me in a band.

VIII.

Hers was the sweetest of sweet faces,
 Hers the tenderest eyes of all!
In her hair she had the traces
 Of a heavenly coronal,
Bringing sunshine to sad places where the sun-
 light could not fall.

IX.

She was fairer than a vision ;
　　Like a vision, too, has flown.
I who flushed at her decision,
　　Lo ! I languish here alone ;
And I tremble when I tell you that my anger
　　was mine own.

X.

Not for her, sweet sainted creature !
　　Could I curse her to her face ?
Could I look on form and feature,
　　And deny the inner grace ?
Like a little wax Madonna she was holy in the
　　place.

XI.

And I told her, in mad fashion,
　　That I loved her,—would incline
All my life to this one passion,
　　And would kneel as at a shrine ;
And would love her late and early, and would
　　teach her to be mine.

XII.

Now in dreams alone I meet her
　　With my lowly human praise :
She is sweeter and completer,
　　And she smiles on me always ;
But I dare not rise and greet her as I did in
　　early days.

→⚬-⚬←

BEETHOVEN AT THE PIANO

I.

SEE where Beethoven sits alone—a dream of
    days elysian,
A crownless king upon a throne, reflected in a
    vision—
The man who strikes the potent chords which
    make the world, in wonder,
Acknowledge him, though poor and dim, the
    mouth-piece of the thunder.

II.

He feels the music of the skies the while his
    heart is breaking;
He sings the songs of Paradise, where love has
    no forsaking ;
And, though so deaf he cannot hear the tem-
    pest as a token,
He makes the music of his mind the grandest
    ever spoken.

III.

He doth not hear the whispered word of love
    in his seclusion,
Or voice of friend, or song of bird, in Nature's
    sad confusion ;
But he hath made, for Love's sweet sake, so
    wild a declamation
That all true lovers of the earth have claim'd
    him of their nation.

IV.

He had a Juliet in his youth, as Romeo had
    before him,
And, Romeo-like, he sought to die that she
    might then adore him ;
But she was weak, as women are whose faith
    has not been proven,
And would not change her name for his—
    Guicciardi for Beethoven.

V.

O minstrel, whom a maiden spurned, but whom
    a world has treasured !
O sovereign of a grander realm than man has
    ever measured !
Thou hast not lost the lips of love, but thou
    hast gain'd, in glory,
The love of all who know the thrall of thine
    immortal story.

VI.

Thou art the bard whom none discard, but
    whom all men discover
To be a god, as Orpheus was, albeit a lonely
    lover ;
A king to call the stones to life beside the roar-
    ing ocean,
And bid the stars discourse to trees in words of
    man's emotion.

VII.

A king of joys, a prince of tears, an emperor of
    the seasons,
Whose songs are like the sway of years in
    Love's immortal reasons ;

A bard who knows no life but this : to love and
    be rejected,
And reproduce in earthly strains the prayers of
    the elected.

VIII.

O poet heart ! O seraph soul ! by men and
    maids adorèd !
O Titan with the lion's mane and with the
    splendid forehead !
We men who bow to thee in grief must tremble
    in our gladness,
To know what tears were turned to pearls to
    crown thee in thy sadness.

IX.

An Angel by direct descent, a German by
    alliance,
Thou didst intone the wonder-chords which
    made Despair a science,
Yea, thou didst strike so grand a note that, in
    its large vibration,
It seemed the roaring of the sea in nature's
    jubilation.

X.

O Sire of Song ! Sonata-King ! Sublime and
    loving master ;
The sweetest soul that ever struck an octave in
    disaster ;
In thee were found the fires of thought—the
    splendours of endeavour,—
And thou shalt sway the minds of men for ever
    and for ever !

A VETERAN POET

I KNEW thee first as one may know the fame
  Of some apostle, as a man may know
  The mid-day sun far-shining o'er the snow.
I hail'd thee prince of poets! I became
Vassal of thine, and warm'd me at the flame
  Of thy pure thought, my spirit all aglow
  With dreams of peace, and pomp, and lyric
    show,
And all the splendours, Master! of thy name.
But now, a man reveal'd, a guide for men,
  I see thy face, I clasp thee by the hand;
  And though the Muses in thy presence stand,
There's room for me to loiter in thy ken.
O lordly soul! O wizard of the pen!
  What news from God? What word from
    Fairyland?

EXTRACTS FROM

THE ROYAL MARRIAGE ODE

July 5th, 1893

I.

WINTER has gone,—
The world is young again!
The jocund hours, careering in the train
Of this imperial day, will travel on
To hope and joy's fulfilment in the Land.
And hark! the cannon,—hark! the cannon's
  roar,

Nineteenth Century.

As loud as waves that lash the rocky strand
When storm-delights are near,
And when the winds, exultant evermore,
Unfurl the glorious flag that we revere !

II.

Ring out the Joy-Bells on the quickening air,
And let allegiance wait on ecstasy !
The world's in tune, to-day, with our desire,
And mirth and music make the morning fair,
And isle responds to isle, and sea to sea,
And all our thoughts aspire
To one majestic theme, and one acclaim,
In Love's transcendent name
That has for wreath a flame,
And is the rapt controller of the lyre.

· · · · · ·

VI.

There's not a flower alive, and not a bird,
And not a woodland thing,
And not a wandering brook that is not stirred
With some solution of sweet euphony,
As if the key-note of the golden spring
Were tossed from choirs above,
And tuned to concert-pitch to rhyme with love !
The very fields, a-shimmering all the morn,
Are proud to wave their poppies in the corn
As if they, too, had banners and were free.
The lark, alert in Heaven, is loud with song,
And trills of summer's prime,
And pairing-days in England's fair domain,
And trysting-hours, gone by, that come again,

And love's delight that knows not any wrong :
So sweet it is to dream of sorrows slain !
And how the breezes, wandering o'er the thyme,
Do seem to rhapsodise
On faith that lives, and hope that never dies,—
As if the fields were richer for the ode
Of their true singer on his sunward road,
And soon would tempt him back from out the
    blue ;
The cowslips huddle close, as gossips do,
Who talk of bridal hours, and wedding-gear,
Whereof the thoughts entrance
The souls of men and maids throughout the
    year ;
The trees are touched with sense of some
    romance,
And every flow'ret has a look of cheer
Whereof the birds take heed ;
And like a moving army on the mead,
The miles of grass are all astir with life,
A million blades uplifted in the sun,
As if for battles won
In some delicious daintiness of strife !
And so in towns and cities, far and near,
The flowers of joy, the posies of delight
Are worn as trophies, and, with little sighs,
Looked at by lovers when they guess aright
The reasons of the redness of the rose,
And why the lily trembles, and is white ;
And why the breeze is welcome, when it blows
A word of wonder from a fairy shore
Where Love is blind no more,
But sees all things, and truly, with glad eyes !

    •   •   •   •   •   •

Nineteenth Century.

XI.

It is the type of May that here to-day
With lustrous eyes and lips that seem to say
" God keep the Kingdom safe " !—it is the May,
The gemmed, the joyous May that on him
    smiles,—
The Loved One of the Isles
Whose fame shall none dispute or disavow
As, with her radiant, diamond wreathèd brow,
She bends from left to right,
And right to left, with love-assenting eyes,
In this cortège of wonder and delight,
While shouts on shouts arise
To greet the spouse of England's future king ;
The sight of her is sweeter than the sight
Of hawthorn-buds that make the meadows
    bright,
And fringe the frondal garments of the year ;
And now July is here
We know 'twas Heaven that brought us back
    the Spring
To make us glad to-day ;
And while the amorous bells about us ring,
We dream of flowers that grow for us in May,—
The mignonette that loves a lonely spot.
The jasmine pale, the blue forget-me-not
That looks with little eyes all down the lanes
To watch for happy swains ;
And daisies, with the wimples they have on,
That drink the dews and drowsiness of dawn ;
And that fair flower of youth,
The rose of York,—the white rose of the
    hedge,—
That was a soldier's pledge,

And is, to-day, a sailor's, as we know,
With petals like the snow,—
The spotless symbol of a Prince's truth.

    •   •   •   •   •   •

XIII.

Ruler of Heaven, that with a lightning-flash
Dost eye the welkin, and, from star to star,
Dost count the myriads of mortality,
And art for ever, as Thine angels are,
Unseen of men this side the sunset-bar,
And hast Thy footfall on the tidal sea
In hours of calm, and when the tempests clash,—
O Thou that art unfailing in Thy might,
And hast, by day and night,
A Father's love, unfaltering to the end,
For all who sky-ward tend,
And evermore art prompt in Thy decrees,—
Look down on us, Thy people, and on these,
The children of the children of the Throne,
For whom the bells intone
The loudest, proudest, most ecstatic notes
That e'er from molten throats
Have flung entrancement on the fields and
    bowers,
And towns and topmost towers,
Of this our land of love and enterprise !
O Thou that hast Thy sanctum in the skies
Beyond the spaces where the planets meet,
And watchest all Thy creatures from above ;
For countless æons that to thee are hours,
Or minutes merely, or a pulse's beat
Betwixt the yea and nay of acted thought.—

Nineteenth Century.

O Thou that in the fulness of fair love
Dost make from out the nothingness of nought
The surging millions of mortality,
And hast the thunder for Thine ancient voice,
And for Thy silence, death,—
And for the flux and influx of Thy breath
The rush and roll of ages that rejoice,—
Bless Thou, this day, the realm, as in the past ;
Bless and defend our Kingdom of the Sea,
That all who turn to Thee
May find their solace here, from first to last,
And rout the foes of Freedom and of Right,
Who launch, in our despite,
The lie that's merged in mockery of all good.
Disperse them, Mighty God, with all their
        brood,
And make them fall,—as fall in hurricanes
The doomed, unbending trees,—
That, in the years to come, none such may
        sound
Their traitorous tocsin-bell on English ground,
Whereon, to-day, are heard the lilting strains
Of glory's interlude,
With Love's full chorus on the summer breeze !

Philip Bourke Marston

MY GARDEN

O MY Garden, full of roses,
  Red as passion and as sweet,
Failing not when summer closes,
  Lasting on through cold and heat !

O my Garden, full of lilies,
  White as peace, and very tall,
In your midst my heart so still is
  I can hear the least leaf fall !

O my Garden, full of singing
  From the birds that house therein,
Sweet notes down the sweet day ringing
  Till the nightingales begin !

WHAT THE ROSE SAW

THE ROSE.

O LILY sweet ! I saw a pleasant sight.

THE LILY.

Where saw you it, and when?

Dainty Poems.

THE ROSE.

Here, when the Night
Lay calmly over all and covered us,
And no wind blew, however tremulous,
I heard afar the light fall of her feet,
And murmur of her raiment soft and sweet.

THE LILY.

What said she to thee when she came anear?

THE ROSE.

No word; but o'er me bent till I could hear
The beating of her heart, and feel her blood
Swell to a blossom that which was a bud.
Alas! I have no words to tell the bliss
When on my trembling petals fell her kiss;
Sweeter than soft rain falling after heat,
Or dew at dawn, was that kiss, soft and sweet.
Then fell another shadow on the ground,
And for a little space there was no sound.
I knew who stood beside her, saw his face
Shining and happy in that happy place;
I knew not what they said; but this I know,
They kissed and passed: where think you they
        did go?

THE ROSE'S DREAM

I.

O SISTERS ! when last night so well you slept,
I could not sleep ; but through the silent air
I looked upon the white moon, shining where
No scent of any rose can reach, I know.
And as I looked adown the path there crept
A little trembling, restless Wind, and lo !
As near it came, I said : " O little Breeze
Thou hast no strength wherewith to stir the
        trees,
What dost thou in this place?" It only sighed,
And paused a little ere it thus replied :—

II.

"I am the Wind that comes before the rain
Which, even now, bears onward from the
        west,—
The rain that is as sweet to you as rest.
When all the air about the day lies dead,
And the incessant sunlight grows a pain,
Then by the cool rain are you comforted.
O happy Rose, that shall not live to see
This summer garden altered utterly,
You know not of the days of snow and ice,
Nor know the look of wild and wintry skies."

III.

Then passed the Wind ; but left me very sad,
For I began to think of days to come,
Wherein the sun should fail and birds grow
        dumb,
And how this garden then should look, indeed.

Nineteenth Century.

And as I thought of all, such fear I had
I cried to you, asleep, though none would heed.
And so I wept, though none might see me weep,
Till came the Wind again, and bade me sleep,
And sang me such a small, sweet song that soon
I fell asleep while looking on the moon.

IV.

And as I slept I dreamed a fearful dream.
It seemed to me that I was standing here:
The sky was sunless, and I saw anear
All you, my sisters, lying dead and crushed.
I could not hear the music of the stream
That runs hard by, when suddenly there rushed
A giant Wind adown the garden walk,
And all the great old Trees began to talk
And cried, "what does the Rose here! Bid
    her go,
Lest buried she should be in coming snow."

V.

I strove to move away, but all in vain ;
And, flying, as it passed me cried the Wind :
" O foolish little Rose, and art thou blind ?
Dost thou not see the snow is coming fast ?'
And all the swaying Trees cried out again :
" O foolish Rose, to tarry till the last ! "
Then came a sudden whirl, a mighty noise,
As every tree that lives had found a voice ;
And I was borne away, and lifted high
As birds that dart in summer through the sky.

VI.

And then the great Wind fell away ; and so
I felt that I was whirling down and down,
Past trees that strove, with branches bare and
    brown,
To catch me as I fell ; and all they cried :
"She must be buried in the cold deep snow ;
Ah, would she had like other roses died ! "
Then, as I thought to drop, I woke to find
The cool rain falling on me, and the Wind
Singing a rainy song among the trees,
Wherein the birds were building at their ease.

VII.

FIRST FLOWER.

A fearful dream indeed, and such an one
As well may make you sad for days to come.

SECOND FLOWER.

A sad, strange dream !

THE ROSE.

Why is the Lily dumb?

THE LILY.

Too sad the dream for me to speak about !

THE ROSE.

I fear this night the setting of the sun.

A TREE.

Nay, when the sun goes in, the stars come out.
You shall not dream, Rose, such a dream again ;
Forget it now in listening to the rain.

Nineteenth Century.

THE ROSE.

I would the Wind had never talked to me
Of things that I shall never live to see.

—>§—§<—

THE FLOWER AND THE HAND

I.

JUST AFTER NIGHTFALL.

I HEARD a whisper of roses,
  And light white Lilies laugh out:
"Ah! sweet when the evening closes,
  And stars come looking about;
How cool and good it is to stand,
Nor fear at all the gathering hand!"

II.

"Would I were red!" cried a White Rose.
  "Would I were white!" cried a red one;
"No longer the light Wind blows,
  He went with the dear, dead sun.
Here we forever seem to stay;
And yet a sun dies every day."

III.

A LILY.

"The sun is not dead, but sleeping,
  And each day the same sun wakes;
But when stars their watch are keeping,
  Then a time of rest he takes."

MANY ROSES TOGETHER.

" How very wise these Lilies are !
They must have heard Sun talk with Star ! "

IV.

FIRST ROSE.

" Pray, then, can you tell us, Lilies,
    Where slumbers the Wind at night,
When the Garden all round so still is,
    And brimmed with the Moon's pale light?"

A LILY.

" In branches of great trees he rests."

SECOND ROSE.

" Not so ; they are too full of nests."

FIRST ROSE.

" I think he sleeps where the grass is ;
    He there would have room to lie.
The white Moon over him passes ;
    He wakes with the dawning sky."

MANY LILIES TOGETHER.

" How very wise these Roses seem,
Who think they know, and only dream ! "

VI.

FIRST ROSE.

" What haps to a gathered flower?"

SECOND ROSE.

"Nay, sister, now who can tell?
Not one comes back for an hour,
   To say it is ill or well.
I would with such an one confer,
To know what strange things chanced to her.'

VII.

FIRST ROSE.

"Hush! hush! now the Wind is waking—
   Or is it the Wind I hear?
My leaves are thrilling and shaking—
   Good-bye; I am gathered, my dear!
Now, whether for my bliss or woe,
I shall know what the plucked flowers know!"

———⟡———

GARDEN FAIRIES

KEEN was the air, the sky was very light,
Soft with shed snow my garden was, and white;
And walking there, I heard upon the night
      Sudden sound of little voices,—
      Just the prettiest of noises.

It was the strangest, subtlest, sweetest sound;
It seemed above me, seemed upon the ground,
Then swiftly seemed to eddy round and round;
      Till I said: "To-night the air is
      Surely full of garden fairies."

And all at once it seemed I grew aware
That little shining presences were there,
White shapes and red shapes danced upon the
      air ;
    Then a deal of silver laughter ;
    And such singing followed after

As none of you, I think, have ever heard,
More soft it was than note of any bird,—
Note after note, most exquisitely deferred,
    Soft as dew-drops when they settle
    In a fair flower's open petal.

"What are these fairies?" to myself I said ;
For answer, then, as from a garden's bed,
On the cold air, a sudden scent was shed,—
    Scent of lilies, scent of roses,
    Scent of summer's sweetest posies.

And said a small sweet voice within my ear :
" We flowers that sleep through winter, once a
      year
Are by our flower queen let to visit here,
    That this fact may duly flout us—
    Gardens can look fair without us.

" A very little time we have to play ;
Then must we go, oh ! very far away,
And sleep again for many a long, long day,
    Till the glad birds sing above us,
    And the warm Sun comes to love us.

" Hark what the roses sing, now, as we go ! "
Then very sweet and soft, and very low,—
A dream of sound across the garden snow,—
    Came the sound of Roses singing
    To the Lily-bells' faint ringing.

Nineteenth Century.

ROSES' SONG

" Softly sinking through the snow,
   To our winter rest we go ;
   Underneath the snow to house
   Till the birds be in the boughs,
   And the boughs with leaves be fair,
   And the sun shine everywhere.
   Softly through the snow we settle,
   Little snowdrops press each petal.
   Oh ! the snow is kind and white,
   Soft it is, and very light ;
   Soon we shall be where no light is,
   But where sleep is, and where night is,—
   Sleep of every wind unshaken
   Till our summer bids us waken."

Then toward some far-off goal that singing
      drew,
Then altogether ceased ; more steely blue
The blue stars shone ; but in my spirit grew
   Hope of summer, love of roses,
   Certainty that sorrow closes.

SUMMER CHANGES

Sang the Lily and sang the Rose,
Out of the heart of my garden close :
   "O joy, O joy of the summer tide !"
Sang the Wind, as it moved above them,
   " Roses were sent for the Sun to love them,
   Dear little buds, in the leaves that hide !"

. Sang the Trees as they rustled together :
   "O the joy of the summer weather !
   Roses and Lilies, how do you fare ? "
Sang the Red Rose, and sang the White :
   "Glad we are of the Sun's large light,
   And the songs of the birds that dart through
      the air."

Lily, and Rose, and tall green Tree,
Swaying boughs where the bright birds be,
   Thrilled by music, and thrilled by wings,
How glad they were on that summer day !
Little they recked of cold skies and grey,
   Or the dreary dirge that a Storm-Wind sings !

Golden butterflies gleam in the sun,
Laugh at the flowers, and kiss each one ;
   And great bees come, with their sleepy tune,
To sip their honey and circle round ;
And the flowers are lulled by that drowsy sound,
   And fall asleep in the heart of the noon.

A small white cloud in a sky of blue :
Roses and Lilies, what will they do ?
   For a wind springs up and sings in the trees.
Down comes the rain ; the garden's awake :
Roses and Lilies begin to quake,
   That were rocked to sleep by the gentle breeze.

Ah, Roses and Lilies ! each delicate petal
The wind and the rain with fear unsettle—
   This way and that way the tall trees sway :
But the wind goes by, and the rain stops soon,
And smiles again the face of the noon,
   And the flowers grow glad in the Sun's warm
      ray.

Nineteenth Century.

Sing, my Lilies, and sing, my Roses,
With never a dream that the summer closes.
   But the Trees are old ; and I fancy they tell,
Each unto each, how the summer flies :
They remember the last year's wintry skies ;
   But that summer returns the Trees know well.

Major Charles G. Mayers

MONONA

Heard ye e'er the Indian legend
Of the young Brave, Anonawa?
Sometimes called Ussowan (Arrow),
And at others Machekawa *
He who left the Four-Lake garden,
Left it in its beauty peerless;
Only hunter's weapons taking,
But at heart of danger fearless.
He had hunted to the Eastward,
Where the dense woods live in gloaming:
There he met an Indian stranger,
Far from tribe and nation roaming.
One who in the heat of passion
His opponent dead had smitten;
And the blood-avenging spirit
'Gainst his life the doom had written.
So he fled from home and people;
Life alone but thought of saving;
Safe from that unsparing vengeance,
Every other peril braving.
Mute the meeting of these Indians
Each one knew the other stranger
To his tongue and to his people;

* Strong.

Dainty Poems.

Yet they neither thought of danger.
For the eye of both looked kindly,
Fearlessly, though full of question;
Each as asking of the other
Which should make a first suggestion.
Anonawa made advances
By an open hand extending,
And the stranger sprang to answer,
From his eye the welcome sending.
Hunting many days together,
Faith and friendship yet grew stronger;
As they learned a common language
Interchange of thought grew longer.
Till at length the Indian stranger
Told his friend of the disaster
That had made him flee from vengeance,
Following ever fast and faster.
Told him of the wondrous prairies
Stretching far as eye could measure;
Told him of the mighty mountains
And their yellow golden treasure.
"Thou should'st see the ' Prairie Lily,'
Lovelier than the fairest flower
That doth deck the earth in summer;
Richer than the sunset hour.
Could'st thou win the bright Monona,
Make her meet thy glance with pleasure,
Thou might'st then return in triumph
With thy bride a warrior's treasure!"

Anonawa left his wigwam;
Traversed forests, swam the rivers;
E'en the " Father of the Waters,"
Rushing sea, the land that severs.

Many, many moons he travelled,
Nothing fearing, naught to grieve him ;
Ever hoping, only anxious
That his hopes might not deceive him.
He had left the woods behind him ;
And the prairie undulating
Greeted him like swelling ocean,
All his being dominating.
But at length 'neath spreading branches
Of the willows near a river
From the mid-day sun he sheltered,
Thinking on the future ever.
When there burst upon his vision
Maiden beautiful as Heaven ;
To his gaze enraptured, seeming
Goddess unto Indian given.
And he murmured, almost fearing
He might put to flight the vision,
"Surely thou must be Monona ! "
Anxiously, but with decision.
Then his captive ear drank music
Such as ne'er had silence broken,
When she said, " I am Monona ;
Who art thou my name hast spoken ?"
Then he told her of his journey ;
Told her he had come to hover
Near the lodges of her people ;
Told her he had come to love her.
Told her of the Four-Lake garden,
Of the lakes in beauty glassing
Summer skies, or like clear mirrors—
Tints of fleecy cloudlets passing.
Urged that towards the glorious sun-rise,
She with him would backward travel,

Nineteenth Century.

Promising the forest mazes
Of her path he would unravel.
Long she listened, reading clearly
In his eye a depth of feeling,
True and tender for her welfare,
Love, unknown before, revealing.
Then she answered Anonawa :
"Thou so many suns hast striven,
That Monona of the prairie
To thy wigwam should be given,
I will go with thee, young Hunter,
Leave my people, *all* behind me ;
When the West is red at sunset,
For the path thou'lt ready find me.
I will bring our fleetest horses,
Lest e'er we have crossed the prairie
They o'ertake us ; then thy scalp-lock
Some Ute chief would proudly carry."

Anonawa with Monona
By his side, like spirit creatures,
Pressed their horses all the night long,
Racing with the flashing meteors.
In the morning, 'neath the shelter
Thick that fringed the water courses,
Rest they sought, rest and refreshment,
For themselves and for their horses.
As the young man gazed in rapture,
Breathing words by love suggested,
Pensively Monona listened,
Long his strain was unmolested.
Thus she answered, "Anonawa !
I have seen thee in my dreaming,
Seen thee scan the broad lake's surface

When the morning sun was beaming.
Seen thee standing on the headland,
Life and joy in every feature,
While the fanciful lake mirror,
Giant-like enlarged thy stature.
Seen thee watch until the monarch
Of the clouds came slowly sailing,
Then thine arrow sped like lightning,
Guided by an eye unquailing.
Struck to death the noble eagle,
From his sailing downward swooping,
Plunging in the clear lake's bosom,
Wings outspread but talons drooping."
Thus responded Anonawa:
" Thank the Love that led me to thee,
And awoke within my bosom
Longing to behold and woo thee.
We will marry, not as Indians,
But as the white father teaches,—
He who journeyed from the sun-rise,
And about the white Christ preaches.

On a gentle Sabbath morning,
When the sun in beauty smiling
Kissed the lake—the lovely wonder,
Every glance to her beguiling,
In the water stood Monona,
By her side the pale-face father ;
He had promised to baptise her
And her brave young chief together.
And he asked the Indian maiden,
As she stood—by far surpassing
Every beauteous thing in nature
That the crystal lake was glassing.

Nineteenth Century.

This he asked her: "When I sprinkle
Water on thy head and bless thee,
By what name as new-born daughter
Of our faith, shall I address thee?"
And the lovely maiden answered:
"Father I will bear alone a
Name by which my mother called me;
I will always be Monona.
But if names must needs be mingled,
Father, listen to thy daughter,
Take not thou Monona from me,
But give it unto the water."
And from all the tribe assembled,
Far across the lake was thrown a
Joyous shout of glad approval,
Hailing the fair lake—Monona.

Alice Meynell

REGRETS

As, when the seaward ebbing tide doth pour
  Out by the low sand spaces,
The parting waves slip back to clasp the shore
  With lingering embraces,—

So in the tide of life that carries me
  From where thy true heart dwells,
Waves of my thoughts and memories turn to
      thee
  With lessening farewells;

Waving of hands; dreams, when the day
      forgets;
  A care half lost in cares;
The saddest of my verses; dim regrets;
  Thy name among my prayers.

I would the day might come, so waited for,
  So patiently besought,
When I, returning, should fill up once more
  Thy desolated thought;

And fill thy loneliness that lies apart
  In still persistent pain.
Shall I content thee, O thou broken heart,
  As the tide comes again,

And brims the little sea-shore lakes, and sets
  Seaweeds afloat, and fills
The silent pools, rivers and rivulets
  Among the inland hills?

RENOUNCEMENT

I must not think of thee; and, tired yet
    strong,
  I shun the thought that lurks in all delight—
  The thought of thee — and in the blue
    Heaven's height,
And in the sweetest passage of a song.

Oh, just beyond the fairest thoughts that
    throng
  This breast, the thought of thee waits,
    hidden yet bright;
  But it must never, never come in sight;
I must stop short of thee the whole day long.

But when sleep comes to close each difficult
    day,
  When night gives pause to the long watch I
    keep,
  And all my bonds I needs must loose apart,

Must doff my will as raiment laid away, -
  With the first dream that comes with the first
    sleep,
  I run, I run, I am gathered to thy heart.

—※—

THE POET TO HIS CHILDHOOD

In my thought I see you stand with a path on
    either hand,
—Hills that look unto the sun, and there a
    river'd meadow-land.
And your lost voice with the things that it
    decreed across me thrills,
  When you thought, and chose the hills.

" If it prove a life of pain, greater have I judged
    the gain.
With a singing soul for music's sake, I climb
    and meet the rain,
And I choose, whilst I am calm, my thought
    and labouring to be
  Unconsoled by sympathy."

But how dared you use me so? For you bring
    my ripe years low
To your child's whim and a destiny your child-
    soul could not know.
And that small voice legislating I revolt against,
    with tears.
  But you mark not, through the years.

'' To the mountain leads my way. If the plains
    are green to-day,
These my barren hills are flushing faintly,
    strangely, in the May,
With the presence of the Spring amongst the
    smallest flowers that grow."
  But the summer in the snow?

Do you know, who are so bold, how in sooth
    the rule will hold,
Settled by a wayward child's ideal at some ten
    years old?
—How the human arms you slip from, thoughts
    and love you stay not for,
  Will not open to you more?

You were rash then, little child, for the skies
    with storms are wild,
And you faced the dim horizon with its whirl
    of mists, and smiled,
Climbed a little higher, lonelier, in the solitary
    sun,
  To feel how the winds came on.

But your sunny silence there, solitude so light
    to bear,
Will become a long dumb world up in the
    colder, sadder air,
And the little mournful lonelinesses in the little
    hills
  Wider wilderness fulfils.

And if e'er you should come down to the village
    or the town
With the cold rain for your garland, and the
    wind for your renown,

You will stand upon the threshold with a face
  of dumb desire,
  Nor be known by any fire.

It is memory that shrinks. You were all too
  brave, methinks,
Climbing solitudes of flowering cistus and the
  thin wild pinks,
Musing, setting to a haunting air in one vague
  reverie
  All the life that was to be.

With a smile do I complain in the safety of the
  pain,
Knowing that my feet can never quit their
  solitudes again ;
But regret may turn with longing to that one
  hour's choice you had,
  When the silence broodeth sad.

I rebel *not*, child gone by, but obey you
  wonderingly,
For you knew not, young rash speaker, all you
  spoke, and now will I,
With the life, and all the loneliness revealed
  that you thought fit,
  Sing the Amen, knowing it.

William Morris

SUMMER DAWN

Pray but one prayer for me 'twixt thy closed
    lips;
Think but one thought of me up in the stars.
The summer night waneth, the morning light
    slips,
Faint and grey 'twixt the leaves of the aspen,
    betwixt the cloud-bars,
That are patiently waiting there for the dawn:
Patient and colourless, though Heaven's gold
Waits to flow through them along with the sun.
Far out in the meadows, above the young corn,
The heavy elms wait, and restless and cold
The uneasy wind rises; the roses are dun;
They pray the long gloom through for daylight
    new-born.
Round the lone house in the midst of the corn.
Speak but one word to me over the corn,
Over the tender, bow'd locks of the corn.

THUNDER IN THE GARDEN

When the boughs of the garden hang heavy
    with rain
  And the blackbird reneweth his song,
And the thunder departing yet rolleth again,
  I remember the ending of wrong.

When the day that was dusk while his death
    was aloof
  Is ending wide-gleaming and strange
For the clearness of all things beneath the
    world's roof,
  I call back the wild chance and the change.

For once we twain sat through the hot afternoon
  While the rain held aloof for a while,
Till she, the soft-clad, for the glory of June
  Changed all with the change of her smile.

For her smile was of longing, no longer of glee,
  And her fingers, entwined with mine own,
With caresses unquiet sought kindness of me
  For the gift that I never had known.

Then down rushed the rain, and the voice of
    the thunder
  Smote dumb all the sound of the street,
And I to myself was grown nought but a
    wonder,
  As she leaned down my kisses to meet.

Nineteenth Century.

That she craved for my lips that had craved
    her so often,
  And the hand that had trembled to touch,
That the tears filled her eyes I had hoped not
    to soften
  In this world was a marvel too much.

It was dusk 'mid the thunder, dusk e'en as the
    night,
  When first brake out our love like the storm,
But no night-hour was it, and back came the
    light
  While our hands with each other were warm.

And her smile killed with kisses, came back as
    at first
  As she rose up and led me along,
And out to the garden, where nought was
    athirst,
  And the blackbird renewing his song.

Earth's fragrance went with her, as in the wet
    grass,
  Her feet little hidden were set ;
She bent down her head, 'neath the roses to pass,
  And her arm with the lily was wet.

In the garden we wandered while day waned
    apace
  And the thunder was dying aloof ;
Till the moon o'er the minster-wall lifted his
    face,
  And grey gleamed out the lead of the roof.

Then we turned from the blossoms, and cold
    were they grown :
  In the trees the wind westering moved ;
Till over the threshold back fluttered his gown,
  And in the dark house was I loved.

—⧽ξ·ζ⧼—

THE MESSAGE OF THE MARCH WIND

FAIR now is the spring-tide, now earth lies
    beholding
  With the eyes of a lover, the face of the sun ;
Long lasteth the daylight, and hope is enfolding
  The green-growing acres with increase be-
    gun.

Now sweet, sweet it is through the land to be
    straying
  'Mid the birds and the blossoms and the
    beasts of the field ;
Love mingles with love, and no evil is weighing
  On thy heart or mine, where all sorrow is
    healed.

From township to township, o'er down and by
    tillage
  Fair, far have we wandered and long was the
    day ;
But now cometh we at the end of the village,
  Where over the grey wall the church riseth
    grey.

212

Nineteenth Century.

Here is wind in the twilight; in the white road
  before us
The straw from the ox-yard is blowing about;
The moon's rim is rising, a star glitters o'er us,
  And the vane on the spire-top is swinging in
  doubt.

Down there dips the highway, toward the
  bridge crossing over
  The brook that runs on to the Thames and
  the sea.
Draw closer, my sweet, we are lover and lover;
  This eve art thou given to gladness and me.

Should we be glad always? Come closer and
  hearken:
  Three fields further on, as they told me down
  there,
When the young moon has set, if the March
  sky should darken,
  We might see from the hill-top the great
  city's glare.

Hark, the wind in the elm-boughs! From
  London it bloweth,
  And telleth of gold, and of hope and unrest;
Of power that helps not; of wisdom that
  knoweth,
  But teacheth not aught of the worst and the
  best.

Of the rich men it telleth, and strange is the story
  How they have, and they hanker and grip far
  and wide;

And they live and they die, and the earth and
 its glory
 Has been but a burden they scarce might
 abide.

Hark ! the March wind again of a people is
 telling ;
 Of the life that they live there, so haggard
 and grim,
That if we and our love amidst them had been
 dwelling
 My fondness had faltered, thy beauty grown
 dim.

This land we have loved in our love and our
 leisure
 For them hangs in heaven, high out of their
 reach ;
The wide hills o'er the sea-plain for them have
 no pleasure,
 The grey homes of their fathers no story to
 teach.

The singers have sung and the builders have
 builded,
 The painters have fashioned their tales of
 delight ;
For what and for whom hath the world's book
 been gilded,
 When all is for these but the blackness of
 night ?

How long and for what is their patience abiding ?
 How oft and how oft shall their story be told,

Nineteenth Century.

While the hope that none seeketh in darkness
    is hiding,
  And in grief and in sorrow the world grow-
    eth old?

Come back to the inn, love, and the lights and
    the fire,
  And the fiddler's old tune and the shuffling of
    feet;
For there in a while shall we rest and desire,
  And there shall the morrow's uprising be sweet.

Yet, love, as we wend, the wind bloweth be-
    hind us,
  And beareth the last tale it telleth to-night,
How here in the spring-tide the message shall
    find us;
  For the hope that none seeketh is coming to
    light.

Like the seed of midwinter, unheeded, un-
    perished,
  Like the autumn-sown wheat 'neath the snow
    lying green;
Like the love that o'ertook us, unawares and
    uncherished,
  Like the babe 'neath thy girdle that groweth
    unseen;

So the hope of the people now buddeth and
    groweth,
  Rest fadeth before it, and blindness and fear;
It biddeth us learn all the wisdom it knoweth;
  It hath found us and held us, and biddeth us
    hear:

Dainty Poems.

For it beareth the message : " Rise up on the
    morrow
    And go on your way toward the doubt and
        the strife ;
Join hope to our hope and blend sorrow with
    sorrow,
    And seek for men's love in the short days of
        life."

But lo, the old inn, and the lights and the fire,
    And the fiddler's old tune and the shuffling
        of feet ;
Soon for us shall be quiet and rest and desire,
    And to-morrow's uprising to deeds shall be
        sweet.

Miss Muloch

A MAN'S WOOING

You said last night you did not think,
  In all the world of men,
Was one true lover—true alike,
  In word and deed and pen,

One knightly lover constant as
  The old knights who sleep sound,
Some woman, said you, there might be,
  Not one man faithful found—

Not one man resolute to win,
  Or winning, firm to hold,
The woman, not the women sought,
  Herself and not her gold.

Not one whose noble life and pure
  Had power so to control
To humble loving loyalty,
  Her free but reverent soul,

That she beside him gladly moved
  Both sovereign and slave,
In faith unfettered, homage dear,
  Each claiming what each gave.

And then you dropped your eyelids white,
    And stood a maiden brave,
Proud, sweet, unloving and unloved,
    Descending to the grave.

I let you speak, and never replied,
    I watched you for a space,
Until that passionate glow, like youth,
    Had faded from your face.

No anger shewed I—nor complaint ;
    My heart's beat shook no breath ;
Although I knew that I had found
    Her who brings life or death.

The woman true as life or death,
    The love strong as these twain,
Against which seas of mortal fate
    Beat harmlessly in vain.

" Not one true man," I hear it still,
    Your voice's clear, cold sound,
Upholding all your constant swains
    And good knights underground.

" Not one true lover," woman, turn,
    I love you, words are small,
Life speaks plain, this time thirty years
    Perhaps you may know all.

I seek you, you alone I seek :
    All other women fair,
Or wise, or good, may go their way,
    Without my thought or care.

Nineteenth Century.

But you I follow day by day,
  And night by night I keep
My heart's chaste mansion lighted where
  Your image lies asleep.

Asleep ! if e'er to wake, He knows who
  Eve to Adam brought,
As you to me, the embodiment
  Of boyhood's dear, sweet thought,

And youth's fond dream, and manhood's hope
  That still half hopeless shone,
Till every bootless vain ideal
  Commingled into one.

You who are so diverse from me
  Yet seem as much my own,
As this my soul which formed apart,
  Dwells in its bodily throne,

Or rather, for that perishes,
  As these our two lives are,
So strangely, marvellously drawn
  Together from afar.

Till week by week, and month by month,
  We liker seem to grow,
As two hill streams flushed with rich rain,
  Each into the other flow.

I swear no oaths, I tell no lies,
  Nor boast I never knew
A love dream—we all dream in youth—
  And waking I found you.

Dainty Poems of the

The real woman whose first touch
  Aroused to highest life
My real manhood, crown it then,
  Good Angel, friend, love, wife.

Imperfect as I am, and you
  Perchance not all you seem,
We two together garner up
  Our past's bright early dream.

Come home, the old tales were not false,
  Yet the new faith is true,
Those saintly souls who made men knights
  Were women such as you.

For the great love that teaches love
  Deceived not ne'er deceives,
And she who most believes in man
  Makes him what she believes.

Come, if you come not I can wait,
  My faith like life is strong,
My will not little, my hope not much,
  The patient are the strong.

Yet come, Ah! come, the years run fast
  And hearths grow swiftly cold,
Hearts too ; but while blood beats in mine
  It holds you and will hold.

And so before you it lies bare,
  Take it or let it lie,
It is an honest heart, and yours
  Till all eternity.

Nineteenth Century.

EVERY DAY HAS ITS DAWN

Every day has its dawn,
  Its soft and silent eve,
Its noontide hours of bliss or bale ;—
  Why should we grieve?

Why do we heap huge mounds of years
  Before us and behind,
And scorn the little days that pass
  Like Angels on the wind?

Each turning round a small sweet face
  As beautiful as near ;
Because it is so small a face,
  We will not see it clear :

We will not clasp it as it flies,
  And kiss its lips and brow ;
We will not bathe our wearied souls
  In its delicious " Now."

And so it turns from us, and goes
  Away in sad disdain ;
Though we would give our lives for it,
  It never comes again.

Yet every day has its dawn,
  Its noontide and its eve :
Live while we live, giving God thanks,
  He will not let us grieve.

YEAR AFTER YEAR.

YEAR after year the cowslips fill the meadows,
    And year after year the skylarks thrill the air,
Year after year in sunshine and in shadows,
    Rolls the world round, love, and finds us as
      we were.

Year after year as sure as birds returning,
    And spring flowers blossoming above the
      wintry mould,
Year after year in joy and mirth and mourning,
    Love we with love's own youth that never
      can grow old.

Sweet heart and lady love, queen of boyish
      passion,
    Strong hope of manhood, content of age
      begun,
Loved in a hundred ways each in a different
      fashion,
    Yet loved supremely, solely as we can love
      but one.

Dearest and bonniest, though blanched those
      curling tresses,
    Though loose clings the wedding-ring to that
      thin hand of thine,
Brightest of all eyes, the eye that love expresses,
    Sweetest of all lips, lips long since kissed by
      mine.
So let the world go on with all its joys and
      sorrows,
    Its mad shouts o'er fancied bliss, its howl o'er
      pleasures past,

That which it calls love's end, to us was love's
    beginning,
  I clasp my arms around thee and love thee
    to the last.

HER LIKENESS

A GIRL, who has so many wilful ways
  She would have caused Job's patience to for-
    sake him :
Yet is so rich in all that's girlhood's praise,
Did Job himself upon her goodness gaze,
  A little better she would surely make him.

Yet is this girl I sing in nought uncommon,
  And very far from angel yet, I trow.
Her faults, her sweetnesses, are purely human ;
Yet she's more lovable as simple woman
  Than anyone diviner that I know.

Therefore I wish that she may safely keep
  This womanhede, and change not, only grow ;
From maid to matron, youth to age, may creep,
And in perennial blessedness, still reap
  On every hand of that which she doth sow.

PLIGHTED

MINE to the core of the heart, my beauty !
Mine, all mine, and for love, not duty :
Love given willingly, full and free,
Love for love's sake—as mine to thee.

Dainty Poems.

Duty's a slave that keeps the keys,
But Love, the master, goes in and out
Of his goodly chambers with song and shout,
   Just as he please—just as he please.

Mine, from the dear head's crown, brown-
      golden,
To the silken foot that's scarce beholden :
Give to a few friends hand or smile,
Like a generous lady, now and awhile,
   But the sanctuary heart, that none dare win,
Keep holiest of holiest evermore :
The crowd in the aisles may watch the door,
   The high-priest only enters in.

Mine, my own, without doubts or terrors,
With all thy goodnesses, all thy errors,
Unto me and to me alone reveal'd,
   " A spring shut up, a fountain seal'd."
   Many may praise thee—praise mine as thine,
Many may love thee—I'll love them too ;
But thy heart of hearts, pure, faithful, and true,
   Must be mine, mine wholly, and only mine.

Mine !—God, I thank Thee that Thou hast
      given
Something all mine on this side heaven :
Something as much myself to be
As this my soul which I lift to Thee :
   Flesh of my flesh, bone of my bone,
Life of my life, whom Thou dost make
Two to the world for the world's work's sake—
   But each unto each, as in Thy sight, *one.*

The Hon. Roden Noel

BEHOLD an empress-queen, who nobly reigns,
And an ideal womanhood sustains
Upon a throne, who wisely rules by laws,
From long deliberation, clause by clause,
Grown fair, and growing, fed with patriot blood
Of Tyndale, Hampden, Sidney, and the good
Martyred, unnamed illustrious multitude.
Her fifty years of dedicated toil
To all self-pleasing tyrants are a foil,
Who only nurse their poor prerogative,
Whether the starving people die, or live.
Her large, full heart goes forth to all that
    mourn,
Itself, alas! wrung, lacerate, and torn.
Our monarch hath a grander coronet
Than any mighty predecessor yet,
With many a subject people's jewel set.
First, orient India, fount of morning's beam,
Realm of Avâtar, and the wondrous dream!
Australia, young with earth's glad primal
    power,
Who weaves weird visions in her lonely bower,

Arms for defence her well-knit, stalwart sons,
And launches navies, iron-mouthed with guns,
To assure the Mother-mistress of the seas
Dominion more unchallenged over these !
In you, blithe land of long lake, frost, and fur,
Vast volumed waters of St Lawrence pour
Their foaming thunders with an ocean roar !
All ye sent children armed for many a mile,
To help us nobly by Egyptian Nile.
Court gentle Peace ! and yet be well prepared !
Without our England ill the world had fared !
Arm ships and soldiers ! ill may they be spared !
Distrust world-citizens, who fain would loose
Thine argent armour, deemed of no more use !

And thou, dark Afric's tempest-beaten Cape,
Around whom Gama dared his course to shape,
Sublime sea-comrade of Columbus bold,
By perilous water-ways unknown of old,
Thou, in the crown a diamond-beaming star,
Art sending sons to jubilee from far !

The pageant of her triumph proudly shone
With warriors, led erst by Wellington,
And that Black-armoured Prince ; red, sable,
      grey ;
Plumed horsemen, helmed, with steel and
      colour gay,
Swart Indian jewelled, in dim gold array ;
Erect Colonials, powerful of frame,
With nation-founding faces, known to fame ;
From every quarter of the world her guard !
Whose people throng the chariot way; they ward
Her throne from danger ; love is great reward.
Bending with royal grace and beaming eye,
Moves the good queen, whose name is Victory.

Nineteenth Century.

The stately triumph of her glory moves
With loud acclaim, upborne by all the loves
Of all the people ; kings and princes ride,
Her escort, with no ill-beseeming pride ;
Her chariot rolls, surrounded by her sons,
Of whom the nobler, grander port he owns,
Who wedded England's daughter ; who will be
Magnanimous Emperor in Germany ;
He, though great empire his mild rule embrace,
Hath character more lofty than his place.
   Here towering with eagle-crested casque,
Face, form, proclaim one born for his high
    task.
He, a more gentle, just, God-fearing Saul,
Hath waged grim conquering battle with the
    Gaul ;
Will wage a deadlier with the dire disease
That lays him low ; yet, scorning his own ease,
Conquereth here too ; patient, cheerful, brave,
While borne in strong midmanhood to the
    grave,
Bends calm composed eyes on the public good,
Who in his long death helps the multitude,
Country, and well-beloved ; who will not
    swerve,
For if Death numbs the right hand, left will
    serve ;
But when one symptom ''apathy'' they named,
Then all divined that Death at length had
    claimed.   •
If to the lover his dear world grew dim,
A Light and Hope of Europe quenched in him !
Alas ! for her, to whom he gave white heather,
In Caledonia, in blue lover's weather !

He lies in state, he lies in his long rest;
And she hath laid the sere wreath on his breast,
Laurel, wherewith she crowned her Paladin,
In war proved, as in peace, a king of men.
    Our queen moves royally to Westminster.
Fortune hath dealt in gracious mood with her.
Yet an irreparable bereavement laid
A scathing hand upon her heart! Snows
    weighed
Heavily, fallen from care-laden years !
Changed, since that early hour of April tears,
When young-winged Morning in the minster
    shone,
Illumed with Heaven her, wearing earthly
    crown ;
Changed, since her marrying the wise prince
    she lost,
Before chill autumn, and the winter frost ! . . .
    But the broad highway laughs with various
    hue,
That seems to pour from forth aerial blue :
Roof, balcony, door, window, all the street
Teem with a happy people, fain to greet
Her, whom the loyal, glad, tumultuous sound
Doth welcome, Love's loud answering rebound
From her Love-loyal reign, re-echoing
    round ! . . .
Yet if this monarch were not good and just,
To Heaven the pageantry were only dust.

Nineteenth Century.

DYING

They are waiting on the shore
  For the bark to take them home;
They will toil and grieve no more;
  The hour for release hath come.

All their long life lies behind,
  Like a dimly blending dream;
There is nothing left to bind
  To the realms that only seem.

They are waiting for the boat,
  There is nothing left to do;
What was near them grows remote,
  Happy silence falls like dew;
Now the shadowy bark is come,
And the weary may go home.

By still water they would rest,
  In the shadow of the tree;
After battle sleep is best,
  After noise tranquillity.

LOVE—TO A.

As of old the wildered dove,
  Wandering over waters dark,
Finding neither fount nor grove,
  Sought shelter in her home, the ark.

Dainty Poems.

So my little one, my love,
   Turns my restless heart to thee,
Weary, wheresoe'er she rove
   O'er the inhospitable sea.

Time hath linked us heart to heart
   With links of mutual memory,
Of gentle power if aught would part
   To bind us close until we die.

If the world arise to sever,
   Steals a tiny spirit-hand,
Glides to re-unite us ever,
   From the holy silent land.

Find the birthplace of sweet Love ;
   All our fairest gifts may go,
Yet will he immortal prove,
   Fairest of all gods we know !

Find his nest within the grove
   Of mystic manifold delight,
Though all the summer leaves remove,
   He will abide through winter's night ;
Unsearchable the ways of Love !
   Though all the singing choirs be gone,
   Love himself will linger on.

Discover hidden paths of love,
   Explain the common miracle,
Dear abundant treasure-trove,
   Celestial springs in earthly well,
   In human vase Heaven's ænomel !

Sir Noël Paton

A SKETCH IN WATER-COLOURS

(*To a Friend in the South*)

Rain, rain, rain! and the wind's in the east!
It snarls, and snaps like a baited beast,
A baffled lawyer, or slighted priest.

And rain and wind through doorway and rent
Drift, sift, and whistle into my tent
Of memory's dead leaves redolent.

The ink is mildewed, the paper's damp,
There's a crick in my neck, and my legs have
    cramp.
Inside there's a puddle—outside a swamp;

A swamp, a ditch, and a scraggy hedge,
A bit of ploughed land, like a rusty wedge
Stuck in between clumps of bramble and sedge;

A tireless wheel, a gap-tooth harrow,
A bottomless bucket, a legless barrow,
One frog, two snails, and a lop-winged sparrow;

Dainty Poems of the

A rickety paling, some willow scrubs,
A lump of potato-field blotched with dubs,
Where a draggled blackbird is hunting for
    grubs;

A shapeless humplock of last year's peats
In an inky pool, which the thick rain beats
Into ripples—the foreground scene completes.

Beyond there's a sweep of plashy bog,
Through which with heavy footsteps jog
A cowering herd and his cowering dog;

And farther, a reach of fierce grey sea,
Where a tug lies watching under the lee
Of an Isle—unblest with bush or tree.

And over all the white fog trails,
Veiling the hills, as a grave-sheet veils
And yet not hides the dead; while wails

The curlew, like a soul in pain,
To the wailing mew.   And still the rain
Pours down, and the wet wind howls amain.

Such are the sights that meet my view—
The sounds *I* hear the long day through;
While in the balmy south, for *you*,

O happy wanderer! nature wreaths
Herself in loveliness, and breathes
In music; till each day bequeaths

Nineteenth Century

Some golden memory to dower
The morrow,—every joy-wing'd hour
Drops, bee-like, from life's full-blown flower,

Drunken with sweetness ! . . . Yet you say
You'd give it all for one brief day,
However cheerless, damp and grey,

To toss your loose locks to the breeze,
And watch the huge Atlantic seas
Break on the iron Hebrides.

Ah, human nature ! men despise
That they possess, and only prize
And seek what Destiny denies !

But I, with philosophic mind
I spurn these frailties of my kind :
To Fate's decree I'd be resigned,

And either lot contented bear
In south or north—in foul or fair—
So *thou* wert here or *I* were there.

D. G. Rossetti.

THE BLESSED DAMOZEL

THE blessed damozel leaned out
　From the gold bar of Heaven;
Her eyes were deeper than the depth
　Of waters stilled at even;
She had three lilies in her hand,
　And the stars in her hair were **seven**.

Her robe, ungirt from clasp to hem,
　No wrought flowers did adorn,
But a white rose of Mary's gift,
　For service meetly worn;
Her hair that lay along her back
Was yellow like ripe corn.

Herseemed she scarce had been a day
　One of God's choristers;
The wonder was not yet quite gone
　From that still look of hers;
Albeit, to them she left, her day
　Had counted as ten years.

(To one, it is ten years of years.
　. . . Yet now, and in this place,

Dainty Poems.

Surely she leaned o'er me—her hair
    Fell all about my face . . .
Nothing—the autumn-fall of leaves:
    The whole year sets apace.)

It was the rampart of God's house
    That she was standing on ;
By God built over the sheer depth
    The which is Space begun ;
So high, that looking downward thence
    She scarce could see the sun.

It lies in Heaven, across the flood
    Of ether, as a bridge.
Beneath, the tides of day and night
    With flame and darkness ridge
The void, as low as where this earth
    Spins like a fretful midge.

Around her, lovers, newly met
    'Mid deathless love's acclaims,
Spoke evermore among themselves
    Their heart-remembered names ;
And the souls mounting up to God
    Went by her like thin flames.

And still she bowed herself and stooped
    Out of the circling charm ;
Until her bosom must have made
    The bar she leaned on warm,
And the lilies lay as if asleep
    Along her bended arm.

From the fixed place of Heaven she saw
    Time like a pulse shake fierce
Through all the worlds.   Her gaze still strove
    Within the gulf to pierce
Its path ; and now she spoke as when
    The stars sang in their spheres.

The sun was gone now ; the curled moon
    Was like a little feather
Fluttering far down the gulf ; and now
    She spoke through the still weather.
Her voice was like the voice the stars
    Had when they sang together.

(Ah sweet ! even now, in that bird's song,
    Strove not her accents there,
Fain to be hearkened ? when those bells
    Possessed the mid-day air,
Strove not her steps to reach my side
    Down all the echoing stair ?)

'' I wish that he were come to me,
    For he will come," she said.
'' Have I not prayed in Heaven ?—on earth,
    Lord, Lord, has he not pray'd ?
Are not two prayers a perfect strength ?
    And shall I feel afraid ?

" When round his head the aureole clings,
    And he is clothed in white,
I'll take his hand and go with him
    To the deep wells of light ;
As unto a stream we will step down,
    And bathe there in God's sight.

Nineteenth Century.

"We two will stand beside that shrine,
 Occult, withheld, untrod,
Whose lamps are stirred continually
 With prayer sent up to God ;
And see our old prayers, granted, melt
 Each like a little cloud.

"We two will lie i' the shadow of
 That living mystic tree
Within whose secret growth the Dove
 Is sometimes felt to be,
While every leaf that His plumes touch
 Saith His Name audibly.

"And I myself will teach to him,
 I myself, lying so,
The songs I sing here ; which his voice
 Shall pause in, hushed and slow,
And find some knowledge at each pause,
 Or some new thing to know."

(Alas ! we two, we two, thou say'st !
 Yea, one wast thou with me
That once of old.   But shall God lift
 To endless unity
The soul whose likeness with thy soul
 Was but its love for thee ?)

"We two," she said, "will seek the groves
 Where the lady Mary is,
With her five handmaidens, whose names
 Are five sweet symphonies,
Cecily, Gertrude, Magdalen,
 Margaret and Rosalys.

" Circlewise sit they, with bound locks
  And foreheads garlanded ;
Into the fine cloth white like flame
  Weaving the golden thread,
To fashion the birth-robes for them
  Who are just born, being dead.

" He shall fear, haply, and be dumb,
  Then will I lay my cheek
To his, and tell about our love,
  Not once abashed or weak :
And the dear Mother will approve
  My pride, and let me speak.

" Herself shall bring us, hand in hand,
  To Him round whom all souls
Kneel, the clear-ranged unnumbered heads
  Bowed with their aureoles :
And angels meeting us shall sing
  To their citherns and citoles.

" There will I ask of Christ the Lord
  Thus much for him and me :—
Only to live as once on earth
  With Love,—only to be,
As then awhile, for ever now
  Together, I and he."

She gazed and listened and then said,
  Less sad of speech than mild,—
" All this is when he comes."   She ceased.
  The light thrilled towards her, fill'd
With angels in strong level flight.
  Her eyes prayed, and she smil'd.

Nineteenth Century.

(I saw her smile.) But soon their path
   Was vague in distant spheres :
And then she cast her arms along
   The golden barriers,
And laid her face between her hands,
   And wept. (I heard her tears.)

John Ruskin

GOOD-NIGHT

SHE lays her down in beauty's light,—
  Oh, peaceful may her slumbers be !
She cannot hear my breathed " Good-Night,"
  I cannot send it o'er the sea ;
And though my thoughts be fleet and free
  To fly to her with speed excelling,
They cannot speak—she cannot see—
  Those constant thoughts around her dwelling.

Thou planet pale, thou plaintive star !
  Adown whose light the dew comes weeping ;
Thou shinest faint, but wondrous far ;
  Oh ! surely thou beholdst her sleeping.
And though her eye thou canst not see
  Beneath its archèd fringes shrouded,
Thou pallid star ! 'tis well for thee
  That such a lustre is beclouded.

Oh ! haste thee then, thy rays are fleet,
  And   be   thou,   through   her   casement
    gleaming,
A starlight in her slumber sweet,
  An influence of delightful dreaming.

Oh! is there no kind breeze to swell
   Along thy silent looks of light,
And at her slumb'rous ear to tell
   Who sent thee there to say " Good-Night " ?

—>‡‑‡<—

SWISS MAIDEN'S SONG

THE pines are tall, and dark, and wide ;
   The sunbeams through their branches glisten
Upon the mountain's turfy side,
Where cushion-moss is green around.
   There, if you lie and listen,
A voice is heard, a soothing sound
Of waters underneath the ground.

It whispers still—by day, by night ;
   The streamlet flows, I know not where,
By arched rocks concealed from sight.
But still a gentle song you meet,—
   A tinkling in the air
Rising up beneath your feet,
Soft, and low,—mysterious,—sweet.

'Tis like a voice of gentle tone
   Within my heart, from day to day.
I'm by myself, but not alone ;
For still it whispers, whispers there.
   It always makes me gay :—
It talks of all things good or fair ;
—It often talks of young Pierre.

Dainty Poems.

CANZONET

I.

THERE'S a change in the green of the leaf,
  And a change in the strength of the tree;
There's a change in our gladness or grief,—
    There may be a change upon thee,
    But love—long bereft of thee,
    Hath a shade left of thee;
    Swift and pale hours may float
    Past, but it changeth not.

II.

As a thought in a consecrate book,
  As a tint in the silence of air,
As the dream in the depths of the brook,
    Thou art there.
    When we two meet again,
    Be it in joy or pain,
    Which shall the fairest be,—
    Thou—or thy memory?

Schiller

—

THE THREE LESSONS

THERE are three lessons I would write—
   Three words as with a burning pen,
In tracings of eternal light,
   Upon the hearts of men.

Have Hope. Though clouds environ now,
   And gladness hides her face in scorn,
Put thou the shadow from thy brow—
   No night but hath its morn.

Have Faith. Where'er thy barque is driven—
   The calm's disport, the tempest's mirth—
Know this—God rules the host of heaven,
   The inhabitants of earth.

Have Love. Not love alone for one,
   But man as man thy brother call,
And scatter like the circling sun
   Thy charities on all.

Thus grave these lessons on thy soul –
   Faith, Hope, and Love—and thou shalt find
Strength when life's surges rudest roll,
   Light when thou else wert blind.

William Sharp

SCIROCCO

(June)

Softly as feathers
That fall through the twilight
When wild swans are winging
Back to the northward :
Softly as waters,
Unruffled, and tideless,
Laving the mosses
Of inland seas :
Soft through the forest,
And down through the valley,
Light as a breath o'er the pools of the marish,
Still as a moonbeam over the pastures,
Goeth Scirocco.

Warm his breath :
The night-flowers know it,
Love it, and open
Their blooms for its sweetness
Warm the tender low wind of his pinions
Scarce brushing together the spires of the
    grasses.

Dainty Poems.

Ah, how they whisper, the little green leaflets
Black in the dusk or grey in the moonlight :
Ah, how they whisper and shiver, the tremulous
Leaves of the poplar, and shimmer and rustle
When soft as a vapour that steals from the
    marshes
The wings of Scirocco fan silently through them.

Ofttimes he lingers
By ruined nests
Deep in the hedgerows,
And bloweth a feather
In little eddies,
A yellow feather
That once had fluttered
On a breast alive with
A rapture of song :
But slowly ceaseth,
And passeth sadly.
Ofttimes he riseth
Up through the branches
Where the fireflies wander,
Up through the branches
Of oak and chestnut,
And stirs so gently
With sway of his wings
That the leaves, dreaming,
Think that a moonbeam
Only, or moonshine,
Moves through the heart of them.
Upward he soareth
Oft, silently floating
Through the purple ether
Still as the fern-owl over the covert,

Or as allocco haunting the woodland,
Up to the soft curded foam of the cloudlets,
The white dappled cloudlets the south-wind
    bringeth.
There, dreaming, he moveth
Or sails through the moonlight,
Till chill in the high upper air and the silence,
Slowly he sinketh
Earthward again,
Silently floateth
Down o'er the woodlands:
Foldeth his wings and slow through the
    branches
Drifts, scarcely breathing,
Till tired, 'mid the flowers or the hedgerows he
    creepeth,
Whispers alow 'mid the spires of the grasses,
Or swooning at last to motionless slumber
Floats like a shadow adrift on the pastures.

→8-3←

THE SWIMMER OF NEMI

(The Lake of Nemi: September)

WHITE through the azure,
The purple blueness,
Of Nemi's waters
The swimmer goeth.
Ivory-white, or wan white as roses
Yellowed and tanned by the suns of the Orient,
His strong limbs sever the violet hollows;
A shimmer of white fantastic motions

Wavering deep through the lake as he swim-
meth.
Like gorse in the sunlight the gold of his yellow
hair,
Yellow with sunshine and bright as with dew-
drops,
Spray of the waters flung back as he tosseth
His head i' the sunlight in the midst of his
laughter:
Red o'er his body, blossom-white 'mid the blue-
ness,
And trailing behind him in glory of scarlet,
A branch of the red-berried ash of the moun-
tains.
White as a moon-beam
Drifting athwart
The purple twilight,
The swimmer goeth—
Joyously laughing,
With o'er his shoulders,
A gleam in the sunshine
The trailing branch
With the scarlet berries.
Green are the leaves, and scarlet the berries,
White are the limbs of the swimmer beyond
them,
Blue the deep heart of the still, brooding lakelet,
Pale-blue the hills in the haze of September,
The high Alban hills in their silence and beauty,
Purple the depths of the windless heaven
Curv'd like a flower o'er the waters of Nemi.

Dainty Poems of the

(In the Sabine Valleys near Rome)

THROUGH the seeding grass,
And the tall corn,
The wind goes:
With nimble feet,
And blithe voice,
Calling, calling,
The wind goes
Through the seeding grass,
And the tall corn.

What calleth the wind,
Passing by—
The shepherd-wind?
Far and near
He laugheth low,
And the red poppies
Lift their heads
And toss i' the sun.
A thousand thousand blooms
Tost i' the air,
Banners of joy,
For 'tis the shepherd-wind
Passing by,
Singing and laughing low
Through the seeding grass
And the tall corn.

Nineteenth Century.

CLOUDS

(*Agro Romano*)

As though the dead cities
Of the ancient time
Were builded again
In the heights of heaven,
With spires of amber
And golden domes,
Wide streets of topaz and amethyst ways ;
Far o'er the pale blue waste,
Oft purple shadowed,
Of the Agro Romano,
Rises the splendid
City of Cloud.
There must the winds be soft as the twilight,
Invisibly falling when the daystar has wester'd ;
There must the rainbows trail up through the
    sunlight,
So fair are the hues on those white snowy
    masses.
Mountainous glories,
They move superbly ;
Crumbling so slowly,
That none perceives when
The golden domes
Are sunk in the valleys
Of fathomless snow,
Or when in silence,
The loftiest spires
Fade into smoke, or as vapour that passeth
When the hot breath of noon

Dainty Poems.

Thirsts through the firmament.
Beautiful, beautiful,
The City of Cloud,
In splendour ruinous,
With golden domes,
And spires of amber,
Builded superbly
In the heights of heaven.

—→ ֯֯··֯ ֯←—

THE ISLE OF LOST DREAMS

THERE is an Isle beyond our ken,
Haunted by Dreams of weary men.
Grey Hopes enshadow it with wings
Weary with burdens of old things :
There the insatiate water-springs
Rise with the tears of all who weep :
And deep within it, deep, oh deep,
The furtive voice of Sorrow sings.
       There evermore
       Till Time be o'er,
Sad, oh so sad, the Dreams of men
Drift through the Isle beyond our ken.

—→ ֯֯··֯ ֯←—

Percy Bysshe Shelley

THE CLOUD

I.

I BRING fresh showers for the thirsting flowers
  From the seas and the streams ;
I bear light shade for the leaves when laid
  In their noonday dreams.
From my wings are shaken the dews that waken
  The sweet buds every one,
When rocked to rest on their Mother's breast,
  As she dances about the sun.
I wield the flail of the lashing hail,
  And whiten the green plains under ;
And then again I dissolve it in rain,
  And laugh as I pass in thunder.

II.

I sift the snow on the mountains below,
  And their great pines groan aghast ;
And all the night 'tis my pillow white,
  While I sleep in the arms of the Blast.
Sublime on the towers of my skiey bowers,
  Lightning my pilot sits ;
In a cavern under is fettered the Thunder,
  It struggles and howls at fits.

Over earth and ocean with gentle motion
   This pilot is guiding me,
Lured by the love of the Genii that move
   In the depths of the purple sea ;
Over the rills and the crags and the hills,
   Over the lakes and the plains,
Wherever he dream, under mountain or stream,
   The Spirit he loves remains ;
And I all the while bask in heaven's blue smile,
   Whilst he is dissolving in rains.

III.

The sanguine sunrise, with his meteor eyes,
   And his burning plumes outspread,
Leaps on the back of my sailing rack,
   When the morning-star shines dead :
As on the jag of a mountain crag
   Which an earthquake rocks and swings,
An eagle alit one moment may sit
   In the light of its golden wings.
And, when sunset may breathe, from the lit sea
     beneath,
   Its ardours of rest and of love,
And the crimson pall of eve may fall
   From the depth of heaven above,
With wings folded I rest on mine airy nest,
   As still as a brooding dove.

IV.

That orbèd maiden with white fire laden,
   Whom mortals call the moon,
Glides glimmering o'er my fleece-like floor
   By the midnight breezes strewn ;

Nineteenth Century.

Nineteenth Century.

And wherever the beat of her unseen feet,
   Which only the angels hear,
May have broken the woof of my tent's thin roof,
   The stars peep behind her and peer.
And I laugh to see them whirl and flee
   Like a swarm of golden bees,
When I widen the rent in my wind-built tent,—
   Till the calm rivers, lakes, and seas,
Like strips of the sky fallen through me on high,
   Are each paved with the moon and these.

v.

I bind the Sun's throne with a burning zone,
   And the Moon's with a girdle of pearl;
The Volcanoes are dim, and the stars reel and
     swim,
   When the Whirlwinds my banner unfurl.
From cape to cape, with a bridge-like shape
   Over a torrent sea,
Sunbeam-proof, I hang like a roof;
   The mountains its columns be.
The triumphal arch through which I march
   With hurricane, fire, and snow,
When the powers of the air are chained to my
     chair,
   Is the million-coloured bow;
The sphere-fire above its soft colours wove,
   While the moist Earth was laughing below.

VI.

I am the daughter of Earth and Water,
   And the nursling of the Sky:
I pass through the pores of the ocean and shores;
   I change, but I cannot die.

253

For after the rain, when with never a stain
  The pavilion of heaven is bare,
And the winds and sunbeams with their convex
    gleams
  Build up the blue dome of air,
I silently laugh at my own cenotaph,—
  And out of the caverns of rain,
Like a child from the womb, like a ghost from
    the tomb,
  I arise, and unbuild it again.

—✠✠—

TO A SKYLARK

I.

Hail to thee, blithe spirit—
  Bird thou never wert—
That from heaven or near it
  Pourest thy full heart,
In profuse strains of unpremeditated art.

II.

Higher still and higher
  From the earth thou springest:
Like a cloud of fire,
  The blue deep thou wingest,
And singing still dost soar, and soaring ever
  singest.

III.

In the golden lightning
  Of the sunken sun,

O'er which clouds are brightening,
    Thou dost float and run,
Like an unbodied joy whose race is just begun.

IV.

The pale purple even
    Melts around thy flight;
Like a star of heaven
    In the broad daylight,
Thou art unseen, but yet I hear thy shrill
    delight—

V.

Keen as are the arrows
    Of that silver sphere
Whose intense lamp narrows
    In the white dawn clear,
Until we hardly see, we feel, that it is there.

VI.

All the earth and air
    With thy voice is loud,
As, when night is bare,
    From one lonely cloud
The moon rains out her beams, and heaven is
    overflowed.

VII.

What thou art we know not;
    What is most like thee?
From rainbow clouds there flow not
    Drops so bright to see,
As from thy presence showers a rain of
    melody:—

VIII.

Like a poet hidden
In the light of thought,
Singing hymns unbidden,
Till the world is wrought
To sympathy with hopes and fears it heeded
not:

IX

Like a high-born maiden
In a palace tower,
Soothing her love-laden
Soul in secret hour
With music sweet as love which overflows her
bower :

X.

Like a glow-worm golden
In a dell of dew,
Scattering unbeholden
Its aërial hue
Among the flowers and grass which screen it
from the view:

XI.

Like a rose embowered
In its own green leaves,
By warm winds deflowered,
Till the scent it gives
Makes faint with too much sweet these heavy-
wingèd thieves.

Nineteenth Century.

XII.

Sound of vernal showers
   On the twinkling grass,
Rain-awakened flowers,—
   All that ever was,
Joyous and clear and fresh,—thy music doth
     surpass.

XIII.

Teach us, sprite or bird,
   What sweet thoughts are thine :
I have never heard
   Praise of love or wine
That panted forth a flood of rapture so
     divine.

XIV.

Chorus hymeneal
   Or triumphal chant,
Matched with thine, would be all
   But an empty vaunt—
A thing wherein we feel there is some hidden
     want.

XV.

What objects are the fountains
   Of thy happy strain ?
What fields, or waves, or mountains?
   What shapes of sky or plain ?
What love of thine own kind? what ignorance
     of pain?

XVI.

With thy clear keen joyance
  Languor cannot be :
Shadow of annoyance
  Never came near thee :
Thou lovest, but ne'er knew love's sad
  satiety.

XVII.

Waking or asleep,
  Thou of death must deem
Things more true and deep
  Than we mortals dream,
Or how could thy notes flow in such a crystal
  stream ?

XVIII.

We look before and after,
  And pine for what is not :
Our sincerest laughter
  With some pain is fraught ;
Our sweetest songs are those that tell of saddest
  thought.

XIX.

Yet, if we could scorn
  Hate and pride and fear,
If we were things born
  Not to shed a tear,
I know not how thy joy we ever should come
  near.

XX.

Better than all measures
　Of delightful sound,
Better than all treasures
　That in books are found,
Thy skill to poet were, thou scorner of the
　ground !

XXI.

Teach me half the gladness
　That thy brain must know ;
Such harmonious madness
　From my lips would flow
The world should listen then as I am listening
　now.

—⊱⊰—

LOVE'S PHILOSOPHY

THE fountains mingle with the river,
　And the rivers with the ocean ;
The winds of heaven mix for ever
　　　　With a sweet emotion ;
Nothing in the world is single ;
　All things by a law divine
In one another's being mingle—
　　　　Why not I with thine ?

See, the mountains kiss high heaven,
　And the waves clasp one another ;
No sister flower would be forgiven
　　　　If it disdained its brother ;

259

Dainty Poems.

And the sunlight clasps the earth,
   And the moonbeams kiss the sea ;—
What are all these kissings worth,
      If thou kiss not me !

F. L. Stanton

WEARYIN' FOR YOU

Jest a-wearyin' for you,
All the time a-feelin' blue ;
Wishin' for you, wondering when
You'll be comin' home agen ;
Restless—don't know what to do—
 Jest a-wearyin' for you.

Keep a-mopin' day by day ;
Dull—in everybody's way.
Folks they smile and pass along,
Wonderin' what on earth is wrong ;
'Twouldn't help 'em if they knew—
 Jest a-wearyin' for you.

Room's so lonesome, with your chair
Empty by the fireplace there ;
Jest can't stand the sight of it ;
Go out doors and roam a bit ;
But the woods is lonesome, too,—
 Jest a-wearyin' for you.

Comes the wind with soft caress
Like the rustlin' of your dress ;

Dainty Poems.

Blossoms fallin' to the ground
Softly like your footsteps sound ;
Violets like your eyes so blue,—
　Jest a-wearyin' for you.

Mornin' comes.　The birds awake
(Use to sing so for your sake) ;
But there's sadness in the notes
That come thrillin' from their throats !
Seem to feel your absence, too,—
　Jest a-wearyin' for you.

Evenin' falls.　I miss you more
When the dark gloom's in the door ;
Seems jest like you orter be
There to open it for me !
Latch goes tinklin'—thrills me through ;
　Sets me wearyin' for you.

Jest a-wearyin' for you !
All the time a-feelin' blue !
Wishin' for you—wonderin' when
You'll be comin' home agen.
Restless—don't know what to do—
　Jest a-wearyin' for you.

De Witt Sterry

ASHES

Wrapped in a sadly tattered gown,
Alone I puff my briar brown
And watch the ashes settle down
 In lambent flashes ;
While thro' the blue, thick, curling haze,
I strive with feeble eyes to gaze
Upon the half forgotten days
 That left but ashes.

Again we wander through the lane,
Beneath the elms and out again,
Across the rippling fields of grain
 Where softly plashes
A slender brook 'mid banks of fern.
At every sight my pulses burn,
At every thought I slowly turn
 And find but ashes.

What made my fingers tremble so
As you wrapped skeins of worsted snow
Around them, now with movements slow
 And now with dashes?
Maybe 'tis smoke that blinds my eyes,
Maybe a tear within them lies ;
But as I puff my pipe there flies
 A cloud of ashes.

Dainty Poems.

Perhaps you did not understand
How lightly flames of love were fanned,
Ah, every thought and wish I've planned
    With something clashes !
And yet within my lonely den,
Over a pipe, away from men,
I love to throw aside my pen
    And stir the ashes.

Lord de Tabley

LOVE GROWN OLD

I CANNOT kiss thee as I used to kiss;
Time who is lord of love must answer this.
Shall I believe thine eyes are grown less sweet?
Nay, but my life-blood fails on heavier feet.
Time goes, old girl, time goes.

I cannot hold as once I held your hand;
Youth is a tree whose leaves fall light as sand.
Hast thou known many trees that shed them so?
Ay me, sweetheart, I know, ay me, I know.
Time goes, my bird, time goes.

I cannot love thee as I used to love.
Age comes, and little Love takes flight above,
If our eyes fail, have his the deeper glow?
I do not know, sweetheart, I do not know.
Time goes, old girl, time goes.

Why, the gold cloud grows leaden, as the eve
Deepens, and one by one its glories leave.
And if you press me, dear, why this is so,
That this is worth a tear is all I know.
Time flows and rows and goes.

In that old day the subtle child-god came;
Meek were his eyelids, but his eyeballs flame.
With sandals of desire his light feet shod,
With eyes and breath of fire a perfect god
He rose, my girl, he rose.

He went, my girl, and raised your hand and
    sighed,
"Would that my spirit always could abide."
And whispered "Go your ways, and play your
    day,
Would I were god of time, but my brief sway
Is briefer than a rose."

Old wife, old love, there is a something yet
That makes amends, tho' all the glory set;
The after-love that holds thee trebly mine,
Tho' thy lips fade, my dove, and we decline,
And time, dear heart, still goes.

A MADRIGAL

LOVE GIVES ALL AWAY

"And what is Love by nature?"
  My pretty true-love sighs.
And I reply, in feature
  A child with pensive eyes,

An infant forehead shaded
  With many ringlet rings,
And pearly shoulders faded
  In the colour of his wings.

Nineteenth Century.

His ways are those of children
  Who come to be caressed ;
Or as a little wild wren,
  Who fears to leave her nest,—

He is shy ; if one shall beckon,
  He hides, will not obey ;
He spends, and will not reckon,
  For Love gives all away.

He hoards to lavish only,
  And lives in miser way.
Now hermit-like is lonely,
  Now gallant-like is gay.

His palm is always tender ;
  His eyes are rainy gray.
His wage-return is slender,
  For Love gives all away.

His aspect as he muses,
  Is paler than the dead.
He weeps more when he loses,
  Than he laughs when he is fed.

Love at a touch will falter,
  Love at a nod will stay.
But armies cannot alter
  One hair-breadth of his way.

He trembles at a rose-leaf,
  And rushes on a spear.
A thorn-prick and he shows grief,
  But Death he cannot fear.

The tyrant may not quench him,
　　He laughs at prison bars ;
The water-floods may drench him,
　　The fire may give him scars.

Though thou lay chain and fetter
　　On ankle, wrist, and hands,
He will not serve thee better,
　　But soar to unknown lands.

He follows shadow faces
　　Into grave-yards unawares.
He reaps in sterile places,
　　And brings home sheaves of tares.

One tear will heal his anger ;
　　He will wait and watch all day ;
He scoffs at toil and danger,
　　His last crust gives away.

He will strip off his raiment
　　To make his dear one gay,
And will laugh at any payment,
　　Having given all away.

When care his heart engages,
　　And his rose-leaf gathers gray,
He will claim a kiss for wages,
　　And demand a smile for pay.

Nineteenth Century.

SLEEP AND SUNSET

Wait—ay, the hours bring night and night
    brings morn,
The old wheel forces on the waning day.
Wait, till the pale to-morrow shall be born,
    As little gracious, and in turn decay.

Rest is a cloud above the evening sun
    That sees him set, nor fails in steadfast sphere
Peace is a moon that when the stars are done
    Without a twinkle sleeps upon a mere.

Death is the mother and the queen of Peace,
    Against whose breast each little wayward
        child,
Who never rested yet on alien knees,
    Feels her his own and ere he slumbers smiles.

AN IDYLL

The time of pleasant fancies,
    For lass and lad returns
In velvet on the pansies,
    In little rolled-up ferns.

Spring comes and sighs and listen
    For the flute of nuptial bird :
Her primrose mantle glistens,
    But her footfall is not heard.

Dainty Poems of the

She hides in wild-wood places
  To watch the young herb grow :
And on the hyacinth faces
  She writes the word of woe.

And when the year is younger,
  And oak leaves yet are small :
And nestlings gape in hunger,
  And merry crow-boys call :

And on the purple fallows
  The greedy rooks are swaying ;
And, as the morning mellows
  The wenches pass a-maying.

And, as in clouds of roses,
  The orchard breadths expand ,
The chestnut leaf uncloses
  The fingers round its hand.

In glades and groves of beeches
  The pensive lovers rest :
With sighs, in broken speeches,
  Their passion is confessed.

In silence and emotion
  They give themselves away,
To sail Love's restless ocean
  For ever and a day.

For ever and for ever
  They vow for many a year,
When leaves are young : they sever
  When leaves are turning sere.

Nineteenth Century.

Ay me, that Love is faded !
  Heighø, the leaves rush down.
They kissed, in greenwood shaded,
  They part ere woods are brown.

Time, as a boding raven,
  Sails o'er them in his flight :
And on their fairy haven,
  His wing drops dews of blight.

Their morning star was kindled,
  And rode as high as God.
Their evening lamp has dwindled
  To a glow-worm in the sod.

Spring ends, and Love is ended :
  His lute has lost its tone.
And the cadence, once so splendid,
  Dies in a wailing moan.

NUPTIAL SONG

"SIGH, HEART, BREAK NOT

Sigh, heart, and break not ; rest, lark, and
    wake not !
Day I hear coming to draw my Love away.
As mere-waves whisper, and clouds grow
    crisper,
  Ah, like a rose he will waken up with day.

Dainty Poems.

In moonlight lonely, he is my Love only,
  I share with none when Luna rides in gray.
As dawn-beams quicken, my rivals thicken,
  The light and deed and turmoil of the day.

To watch my sleeper, to me is sweeter,
  Than any waking words my Love can say ;
In dream he finds me and closer winds me !
  Let him rest by me a little more and stay.

Ah, mine eyes, close not : and, tho' he knows
     not,
  My lips, on his be tender while you may ;
Ere leaves are shaken, and ring-doves waken,
  And infant buds begin to scent new day.

Fair Darkness, measure thine hours, as treasure
  Shed each one slowly from thine urn, I pray ;
Hoard in and cover each from my lover ;
  I cannot lose him yet ; dear night, delay.

Each moment dearer, true-love, lie nearer,
  My hair shall bind thee lest thou see the ray
My locks encumber thine ears in slumber,
  Lest any bird dare give thee note of day.

He rests so calmly ; we lie so warmly ;
  Hand within hand, as children after play ;—
In shafted amber on roof and chamber
  Dawn enters ; my Love wakens ; here is day.

→§-⅜←

Aubrey de Vere

ODE ON THE ASCENT OF THE ALPS

I.

ALL night as in my dreams I lay,
  The shout of torrents without number
Was in my ears—"Away, away,
  No time have we for slumber !
The star-beams in our eddies play ;
The moon is set : away, away ! "
And round the hills in tumult borne
  Through echoing caves and gorges rocking
The voices of the night and morn
Are crying louder in their scorn,
  My tedious languor mocking.
Alas ! in vain man's mortal limbs would rise
To join in elemental ecstasies.

II.

" But thou, O Muse, our heavenly mate,
Unclogged art thou by fleshly weight !
Ascend ; upbearing my desire
Among the mountains high and higher.
Leap from the glen upon the forest ;
  Leap from the forest on the snow :
And while from snow to cloud thou soarest
  Send back thy song below ! "

Dainty Poems of the

III.

I spake—Behold her o'er the broad lake flying
Like a great Angel missioned to bestow
Some boon on men beneath in sadness lying:
  The waves are murmuring silver murmurs low
    Beneath the curdling wind
Green through the shades the waters rush and roll,
Or whitened only by the unfrequent shoal;
Lo! two dark hills, with darker yet behind,
Confront them, purple mountains almost black,
  Each behind each self-folded and withdrawn
Beneath the umbrage of yon cloudy rack—
    That orange gleam! 'tis dawn!
Onward! the swan's flight with yon eagle's
    blending,
On, wingèd Muse, still forward and ascending!

IV.

That mighty sweep, one orbit of her flight,
Has over-curved the mountain's barrier height:
She sinks, she speeds on prosperous wing pre-
    vailing,
Broad lights below and changeful shadows
    sailing,
Over a vale upon whose breadth may shine
  Not noontide suns alone but suns of even,
Warming the rich fields in their red decline,
  The grey streams flashing with the hues of
    heaven.
In vain those Shepherds call; they cannot wake
  The echoes on this wide and cultured plain
Where spreads the river now into a lake,
  Now curves through walnut meads its
    golden chain,

274

Nineteenth Century.

In-isling here and there some spot
 With Orchard, hive, and one fair cot,
 Or children dragging from their boat
 Into the flood some reverend goat—
O happy valley ! cradle soft and deep
 For blissful life, calm sleep
And leisure, and affections free and wide,
Give me yon plough, that I with thee may bide,
 Or climb those stages hut-bestrown
 Vast steps of summer's mountain-throne
Terrace o'er terrace rising, line o'er line,
Swathed in the light wreaths of the elaborate
 vine.
 On yonder loftiest steep, the last
 From whose green base the grey rocks rise,
In random circle idly cast
 A happy household lies :
Not far there sits the plighted maid ;
Her locks a lover's fingers braid—
Fair, fearless maiden ! cause for fear
Is none, though he alone were near :
Indulge at will thy sweet security !
 He doth but that bold front incline
 And all those wind-tossed curls on thine
To catch from thy fresh lips their mountain
 purity !

v.

Up to lonelier, narrower valleys
 Winds an intricate ravine,
Whence the latest snow-blast sallies
 Through black firs scarce seen.
I hear through clouds the Hunter's hollo—
I hear, but scarcely dare to follow

'Mid chaotic rocks and woods,
Such as in her lyric moods
Nature, like a Bacchante, flings
From half-shaped imaginings;
There lie two prostrate trunks entangled
Like intertwisted dragons strangled;
Yon glacier shines a prophet's robe;
While broken sceptre, throne, and globe
Are strewn as left by rival States
Of elemental Potentates:
Pale floats the mist, a wizard's shroud:
There looms the broad crag from the cloud,
A thunder-graven Sphinx's head, half blind
Gazing on far lands through the freezing wind!

VI.

My song grows smoother, hearing
  A smooth-voiced female hymn
In verse alternate cheering
  The pass above me dim.
Behold them now, a band
Of maids descending hand in hand;
Singing softly, singing proudly
Low-toned anthems echoed loudly,
Martyr sufferings, mountain pleasures
  Grave, religious, sweet affections,
Tuned with notes of ancient measures,
  Linked with patriot recollections!
The land is strong when such as these
  Inspire their lovers and their brothers:
The land is strong with such as these
  Her heroes' destined mothers!
Freedom from every hut
  Sends down a separate root:

Nineteenth Century.

And when base swords her branches cut
  With tenfold might they shoot.
Her Temples are of pine-woods made,
  Not Tyrian gold or Parian stone
With roofs of cedar gem-inlaid :
  There sits she, thence alone
To those dispensing her large love
Who share her solemn feast above,
Nor fear her icy halls or zone
Of clouds with which she girds her own !

VII.

Mount higher, mount higher !
With rock-girdled gyre
  Behind each grey ridge
  And pine-feathered ledge
A vale is suspended ; mount higher, mount
  higher !

From rock to rock leaping
  The wild goats, they bound ;
The resinous odours
  Are wafted around ;
The clouds, disentangled,
  With blue gaps are spangled ;
Green isles of the valley with sunshine are
  crowned.

The birches new budded
  Make pink the green copse ;
From the briar and hazel
  The crystal rain drops ;

As he climbs, the boughs shaking,
Nest-seeking, branch-breaking,
Beneath the white ash-boughs the shepherd-boy
    stops.

How happy that shepherd !
How happy the lass !
How freshly beside them
The pure Zephyrs pass !
Sing, sing ! from the soil
Springs bubble and boil,
And sun-smitten torrents fall soft on the grass

Once more on every turf-clad stage
Peeps forth some household hermitage ;
Once more from tracts serene and high
The young lambs bleat, the dams reply.
From echoing trunks I hear the dash
Of headlong stream or '' Ranz des Vaches.''
Lo ! from thickets lightly springing
    An old church spire ; around its base
Devotions ever upward winging
    That find in Heaven their resting-place ;
Around it grey-haired votaries kneel
    Who look along it to the skies,
And babes with imitative zeal
    Kissing their lip-worn rosaries.
Not soon the mountain Faith grows cold ;
    Yon hamlet is six centuries old !

VIII.
Mount higher, mount higher !
To the cloudland nigher !
To the regions we climb
Of our long-buried prime ;
In the skies it awaits us—Up higher, up higher !

Nineteenth Century

Loud Hymn and clear Pæan
   From the caverns are rolled:
Far below us is Summer;
   We have slipped from her fold;
We have passed like a breath,
To new life without death—
The Spring and our Childhood all round we
   behold.

IX.

What are toils to men who scorn them?
   Perils what to men who dare?
Chains to hands that once have torn them
   Thenceforth are chains of air.
The winds above the snow-plains fleet;
Like them I race with wingèd feet:
My bonds are dropped; my spirit thrills,
A Freeman of the Eternal Hills!

Each cloud by turns I make my tent;
I run before the radiance sent
From every mountain's silver mail
Across dark gulfs from vale to vale:
The curdling mist in smooth career
   A lovely phantom fleeting by
As silent sails through yon pale mere
   That shrines its own blue sky;
The sun that mere makes now its targe,
And rainbow vapours tread its marge;
   A whisper, such as lovers use,
Far off on those still heights was heard;
But here was never sound of bird;
   No wild bee lets its murmur loose

O'er those blue flowers in rocky cleft
Their unvoluptuous eyes that lift
From feathery tufts of spangled moss
Pure as the snows which they emboss.
Lo! like the foam of wintry ocean,
 The clouds beneath my feet are curled :
Dividing now with solemn motion
 They give me back the world.
No veil I fear, no visual bond
In this aërial diamond :
My head o'er crystal bastions bent
'Twixt star-crowned spire and battlement
I see the river of green ice
From precipice to precipice
Wind earthward slow, with blighting breath
Blackening the vales below like death.
Far, far beneath in sealike reach
 Receding to the horizon's rim
I see the woods of pine and beech,
 By their own breath made dim :
I see the land which heroes trod ;
 I see the land where Virtue chose
To live alone, and live to God ;
 The land she gave to those
Who know that on the hearth alone
True Freedom rears her fort and throne.

x.

Lift up not only hand and eye,
Lift up, O man, thy heart on high :
Or downward gaze once more ; and see
How spiritual dust can be !
Then far into the Future dive,
And ask if there indeed survive,

Nineteenth Century.

When fade the worlds, no primal shapes
Of disembodied hills and capes,
Types meet to shadow Godhead forth ;
Dread antitypes of shapes on earth?
O Earth ! thou shalt not wholly die,
    Of some " new Earth " the chrysalis
Predestined from Eternity,
    Nor seldom seen through this ;
On which, in glory gazing, we
Perchance shall oft remember thee,
And trace through it thine ancient frame
Distinct, like flame espied through flame,
Or like our earliest friends, above,
Not lost though merged in heavenlier love—
How changed, yet still the same !

XI.

Here rest my soul, from meteor dreams ;
And thou, my song, find rest.   The streams
That left at morn yon mountain's brow
    Are sleeping with Locarno now.
    Earth seeks perforce from joy release,
    But Heaven in rapture finds her peace.
Gaze on those skies at once o'er all the earth
    Dissolving in a bath of purple dews,
And spread thy soul abroad as widely forth
    Till Love thy soul, as Heaven the snows
        suffuse.
The sun is set—but upwards without end
    Two mighty beams, diverging,
Like hands in benediction raised, extend ;
From the great deep a crimson mist is surging
    The peaks are pyres where Day doth lie
    Like Indian widows, proud to die ;

Strange gleams, each moment ten times
    bright,
Shoot round, transfiguring as they smite
All spaces of the empyreal height ;
Deep gleams, high Words which God to man
    doth speak ;
From peak to solemn peak in order driven
They speed—a loftier vision dost thou seek ?
    Rise then to Heaven !

HUMAN LIFE

Sad is our youth, for it is ever going,
    Crumbling away beneath our very feet ;
Sad is our life, for onward it is flowing,
    In current unperceived because so fleet ;
Sad are our hopes, for they were rich in sowing,
    But tares, self sown, have overtopped the
    wheat ;
Sad are our joys, for they were sweet in blowing,
    And still, O still, their dying breath is sweet :
And sweet is youth, although it hath bereft us
    Of that which made our childhood sweeter
    still ;
And sweet our life's decline, for it hath left us
    A nearer Good to cure an older Ill ;
And sweet are all things, when we learn to
    prize them
    Not for their sake, but His who grants them
    or denies them.

Nineteenth Century.

SORROW

COUNT each affliction, whether light or grave,
God's messenger sent down to thee; do thou
With courtesy receive him; rise and bow;
And, ere his shadow pass thy threshold, crave
Permission first his heavenly feet to lave;
Then lay before him all thou hast: allow
No cloud of passion to usurp thy brow,
Or mar thy hospitality; no wave
Of mortal tumult to obliterate
The soul's marmoreal calmness: Grief should
        be,
Like joy, majestic, equable, sedate;
Confirming, cleansing, raising, making free;
Strong to consume small troubles; to commend
Great thoughts, grave thoughts, thoughts last-
        ing to the end.

—⟩⟨—

A WINTER NIGHT IN THE WOODS

WHEN first the Spring her glimmering
        chaplets wove
This way and that way 'mid the boughs high
        hung
We watched the hourly work, while thrushes
        sung
A song that shook with joy their bowered
        alcove:
Summer came next; she roofed with green the
        grove,

283

And deepening shades to flower-sweet alleys
    clung :
Then last,—one dirge from many a golden
    tongue—
The chiding leaves with chiding Autumn strove.
These were but Nature's preludes.   Last is
    first !
Winter, uplifting high both flail and fan,
With the great forests dealt as Death with man ;
And therefore through their desolate roofs hath
    burst
This splendour veiled no more by earthly bars
Infinite Heaven, and the fire-breathing stars !

→⸫⸪←

ROBERT BROWNING

(*January* 1890)

ι.

Gone from us ! that sweet singer of late days—
Sweet singer should be strong—who tarrying
    here,
Chose still rough music for his themes austere,
Hard-headed, aye, but tender-hearted lays,
Carefully careless, garden half, half maze.
His thoughts he sang, deep thoughts to thinkers
    dear,
Now flashing under gleam of smile or tear,
Now veiled in language like a breezy haze

Nineteenth Century.

Chance-pierced by sunbeams from the lake it
    covers.
He sang man's ways—not heights of sage or
    saint,
Not highways broad, not haunts endeared to
    lovers :
He sang life's bye-ways, sang its angles quaint,
Its Runic lore inscribed on stave or stone,
Song's short-hand strain—its key oft his alone.

II.

Shakespeare's old oak " gnarled and unwedge-
    able "
Yields not so sweet a wood to harp or lyre
As tree of smoother grain ; and chorded shell
Is spanned by strings tenderer than iron wire.
What then ? Stern tasks iron and oak require,
Iron deep-mined, hard oak from stormy fell :
Steel-armed the black ship breasts the ocean's
    swell,
Oak-ribbed laughs back the raging tempest's
    ire.
Old friend, thy song I deem a ship whose hold
Is stored with mental spoils of ampler price
Than Spain's huge galleons in her age of gold,
Or Indian carracks from the isles of spice.
Brave Argosy ! cleave long the waves as now,
And all the sea-gods sing around thy prow !

Ella Wheeler Wilcox

TOGETHER

WE two in the fever and fervour and glow
  Of life's high tide have rejoiced together ;
We have looked out over the glittering snow,
  And knew we were dwelling in Summer
    weather,
For the seasons are made by the heart, I hold,
And not by out-door heat or cold.

We two in the shadows of pain and woe,
  Have journeyed together in dim, dark places,
Where black robed Sorrow walked to and fro,
  And Fear and Trouble with phantom faces
Peered out upon us and froze our blood,
Though June's fair roses were all in bud.

We two have measured all depths, all heights,
  We have bathed in tears, we have sunned in
    laughter,
We have known all sorrows and all delights—
  They never could keep us apart hereafter.
Wherever your spirit was sent I know
  would defy earth—or heaven—to go.

Dainty Poems.

If they took my soul into Paradise,
    And told me I must be content without you,
I would weary them so with my lonesome cries,
    And the ceaseless questions I asked about
        you—
They would open the gates and set me free,
Or else they would find you and bring you to
        me.

Wordsworth

THE DAFFODILS

I WANDERED lonely as a cloud
  That floats on high o'er vales and hills,
When all at once I saw a crowd,
  A host of golden daffodils ;
Beside a lake, beneath the trees,
Fluttering and dancing in the breeze.

Continuous as the stars that shine
  And twinkle on the milky-way,
They stretched in never-ending line
  Along the margin of a bay ;
Ten thousand saw I at a glance,
Tossing their heads in sprightly dance.

The waves beside them danced, but they
  Outdid the sparkling waves in glee :
A poet could not but be gay
  In such a jocund company.
I gazed, and gazed, but little thought
What wealth the show to me had brought.

For oft when on my couch I lie
  In vacant or in pensive mood,
They flash upon that inward eye,
  Which is the bliss of solitude ;
And then my heart with pleasure fills
And dances with the daffodils.

Anonymous

NO UNBELIEF

THERE is no unbelief;
Whoever plants a seed beneath the sod
And waits to see it push away the clod—
He trusts in God.

Whoever says, when clouds are in the sky,—
" Be patient, heart ; light breaketh by and by,"
Trusts the Most High.

Whoever sees, 'neath winter's field of snow,
The silent harvest of the future grow,
God's power must know.

Whoever lies down on his couch to sleep,
Content to lock each sense in slumber deep,
Knows God will keep.

Whoever says, " To-morrow," " The Un-
    known,"
" The Future," trusts that Power alone
He dares disown.

The heart that looks on when the eyelids close,
And dares to live when life has only woes,
God's comfort knows.

There is no unbelief ;
And day by day, and night unconsciously,
The heart lives by that faith the lips deny—
God knoweth why !

Kate E. Bunce

THE IMPS IN THE HEAVENLY MEADOW

(Versified from the German of Baumbach)

To Heaven's Meadows, bright with flowers
    and sunshine,
  The little children go,
When they have had enough of life's sad
    dreaming,
  And leave the earth below.

But as they had not time to learn their lessons
  Before they went away,
There is a school, where all the angel children
  Must work four hours a day.

With golden pencils upon silver tablets,
  They copy fairy tales,
And learn to keep their halos bright and
    shining,
  And sing, and play their scales.

And twice a week they glide with merry
    laughter
  All down the Milky Way,
And homeward in the evening wander softly
  Upon a sunset ray.

Dainty Poems.

But Sunday is the day they love and long for;
   Then all the children go
And play from morn till night within a meadow
   Where flowers in thousands grow.

The meadow is not green, but blue and golden,
   The flowers like dewdrops bright;
When it is night, they burn and glow and
      glisten—
   Then call them stars of light.

Through Heaven's gate they all must pass to
      find it,
   Where Peter with the key
Keeps watch and warns the little angels kindly
   How good they all must be.

They must not fly about or run too quickly,
   Nor go too far away,
And when upon his golden key he calls them,
   Then they must all obey.

     .   .   .   .   .

One day it was so very hot in Heaven
   That good St Peter slept,
And when the little children saw it,
   Away they quickly crept.

Ah! then they ran and flew about with laughter,
   And fluttered far and wide,
So far they wandered that of Heaven's Meadow
   They reached the other side.

They came to where the strong, tall, wooden
    paling
  Shuts all that place away,
Where idle, careless, mischief-loving, naughty,
  The Imps of Darkness stray.

And there the angels stopped, devoutly wishing
  Some opening there might be,
So that they might each one in turn peep
    through it,
  And see what they could see.

But not a chink or hole, for all their seeking,
  No gleam of light pierced through,
So with their little wings outspread and eager,
  Right to the top they flew ;

And looking down they saw with awe and
    wonder,
  Imps all as black as soot ;
Each had two horns and each a tail to play
    with,
  And hoof, instead of foot.

They heard the rustle of the angel feathers,
  They felt the cool sweet air,
And, lifting up their little coal black faces,
  They saw Heaven's children there.

Then with one voice they cried : "Oh ! angel
    children,
  You look so good and fair,
We pray you, let us come up into Heaven
  And play a little there.

Nineteenth Century.

"We will not tweak, nor pull your shining
    feathers
  But be so very good ;
We will not try and steal your little halos,
  But all do as we should."

Then quick they flew away for Jacob's Ladder,
  (Peter was still asleep,)
And placed it safely, where from earth to imp-
    land
  The way was dark and steep.

Then every little imp, with shouts and laughter,
  Helped by an angel's hand,
Scrambled right over the great wooden paling,
  And stood in Heaven's land.

They all, with air sedate and pious faces,
  Discreetly walked around,
Their tails like trains upon their arms up-
    holding,
  And eyes upon the ground.

The little angels fluttered round in rapture,
  And showed the lovely flowers,
And bade them listen to the thrilling voices
  Of birds in Heaven's bowers.

And gently led them by the crystal streamlets,
  Bade them on dewdrops feast,
And showed them where the silver moon was
    rising
  To light them from the east.

Alas ! when all the little demons saw her,
  The moon, so large and round,
They all began to roar, and growl, and gibber,
  And leap from off the ground ;

And mocked the great white moon with ugly
      faces,
  Turned somersaults in air,
And when the angels prayed them cease, in
      terror,
  They vowed they did not care.

They trampled down the grass in Heaven's
      Meadow,
  They tore the flowers about,
And flung them on the earth beyond the paling,
  With gibe, and jeer and shout.

They chased the birds that sang among the
      tree-tops
  And hushed their music sweet,
They pulled the little angel's tender feathers
  And trod upon their feet.

Then to the good St Peter cried the angels
  To help them in their pain,
And if he would but this one time forgive them,
  They would be good again.

Then rose St Peter from his peaceful dreaming—
  An angry saint was he—
He wrung his hands and clasped his head in
      horror,
  And seized his golden key.

Nineteenth Century.

Then blew a mighty blast in wrath upon it :
    Back all the angels flew,
And wide he threw the door of Heaven open,
    And thrust the children through.

And then he called two great and powerful
        angels,
    The strongest of the race,
To chase the little demons out of Heaven,
    And clear the holy place.

They gathered up the little imps in armsful,
    Bore them with mighty stride,
And flung them over the strong wooden paling
    Down on the other side.

And though they fought and lashed their tails
        and whimpered,
    And kicked with might and main,
To Heaven's Meadow, bright with sun and
        flowers,
    They never came again.

For two long months the little angel-children
    Were not allowed to play
Before the door of Heaven in the meadow,
    But stayed in all the day.

And when again they sought the Heavenly
        Meadow
    Each child with humble mind
Must lay aside its little shining halo,
    And leave its wings behind.

     .   .   .   .   .

But all the flowers that on that day of sorrow,
    Flung out and scattered were,
Took root and bloom again in earth's green
        meadows,
    As daisies white and fair.

And in the daisies lies a magic virtue :
    They will the truth impart
To any doubtful maid who seeks their counsel,
    To satisfy her heart.

For if the maid will know the truth or false-
        hood
    Of one who comes to woo,
And pulls each petal as she asks the question,
    The last one will be true !

INDEX.

Index.

Index.

Index.

Index.

Index.

Index.

Index.

WHITEHEAD AND COMBRIDGE, LTD., PRINTERS,
FREDERICK STREET, BIRMINGHAM.